"Amanda, you danced every dance with the same boy. All evening long. You shouldn't have done that. It was improper."

"His name is Jed Langford and it wasn't his fault at all. I *wanted* to be with him. I like him. Oh, Father, I do like him!" Amanda took a breath and the rest came out in a rush. "He'll be at church this morning and I hope we can invite him for lunch after and—You'll see that he's nice and—"

"Amanda, stop! You're certainly not going to have gentlemen callers at your age. I forbid it."

"Not *callers*," she whispered. "Only one. Only Jed."

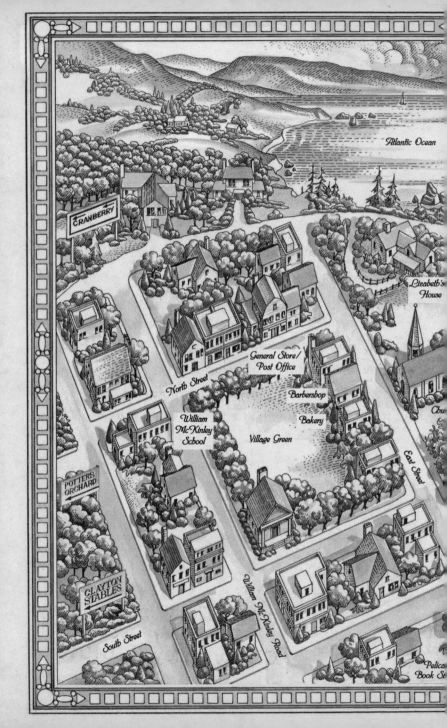

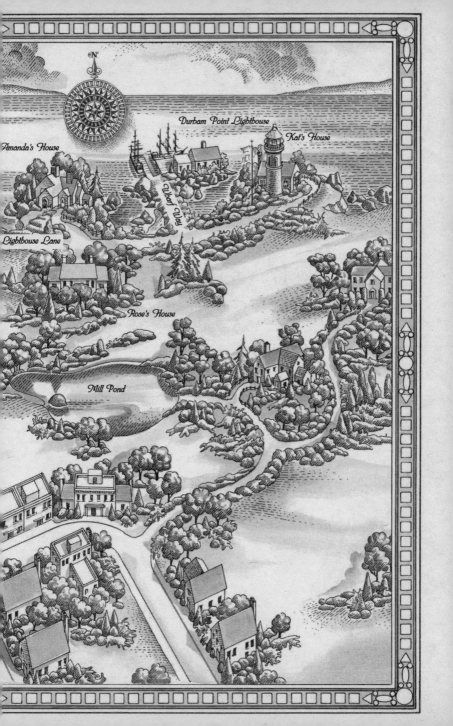

Other books by

THOMAS KINKADE *and* **ERIKA TAMAR**

THE GIRLS OF LIGHTHOUSE LANE

Katherine's Story

Rose's Story

Lizabeth's Story

Amanda's Story

THOMAS KINKADE

The Girls of Lighthouse Lane

Amanda's Story

A CAPE LIGHT NOVEL

By Erika Tamar

Avon Books
An Imprint of HarperCollins*Publishers*

A PARACHUTE PRESS BOOK

Avon is a registered trademark of HarperCollins Publishers.

The Girls of Lighthouse Lane: Amanda's Story
Copyright © 2005 Thomas Kinkade, The Thomas Kinkade Company,
Morgan Hill, CA,
and Parachute Publishing, L.L.C.

Map of Cape Light by Joseph Scrofani

Library of Congress Cataloging-in-Publication Data
Kinkade, Thomas, 1958-
    Amanda's story / by Thomas Kinkade and Erika Tamar. — 1st ed.
        p. cm. — (The girls of Lighthouse Lane ; #4)
        "A Parachute Press book."
    Summary: While living in Cape Light during the years 1905 to 1906, thirteen-year-
old Amanda struggles to obey her widowed father's orders not to see the boy she
loves, despite her angry resentment of her parent's courtship of a local widow.
    ISBN-10: 0-06-054352-3 — ISBN-13:978-0-06-054352-5
    [1. Fathers and daughters—Fiction. 2. Courtship—Fiction. 3. Friendship—
Fiction. 4. Family life—New England—Fiction. 5. New England—History—20th
century—Fiction.] I. Tamar, Erika. II. Title.
PZ7.K6192Am 2005   2004012292
[Fic]—dc22   CIP
                                                                          AC

❖

First Avon edition, 2006

The Girls of Lighthouse Lane

Amanda's Story

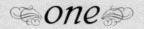 *one*

Saturday night, October 21, 1905

Amanda Morgan paused on the path outside the Hallorans' barn. She smoothed the long skirt of her new burgundy wool dress from the Montgomery Ward catalog and wondered if the boy who stared at her in church would be at the barn dance tonight. No, he didn't even live in Cape Light. . . . But maybe. . . . No, of course not. . . . The thought of seeing him, maybe even *talking* to him, made Amanda jittery.

It would be better, and lots more relaxing, if he wasn't here. Anyway, her father didn't approve of courtship at her age. And more than anything, she wanted to be the perfect model of a minister's daughter and make him proud.

Amanda adjusted her heavy wool shawl so that the pretty crocheted edging at the neckline of her dress would show. She bit her lips and pinched her cheeks to give them color—tricks that her friend Lizabeth had taught her. But Amanda's cheeks were already flushed with excitement. Even from outside, Amanda could hear the toe-tapping music and the fiddler calling, "Swing in the center, then break that pair; lady goes on and gent stays there. . . ."

The last barn dance in Cape Light had been ages ago, after the barn raising for a just-married couple on William McKinley Road. Amanda had been only eleven then. The boys she knew from school had piled up at the refreshment table, competing to see who could eat the most. Not that she'd cared; it had been fun to skip around with her girlfriends and dance the Virginia reel with Father. But now she was thirteen and everything was different.

Amanda scanned the crowd as she entered. No, she didn't see him—and, in spite of herself, she felt a stab of disappointment.

He had started coming to Father's church a month ago and then he showed up every Sunday. He was startlingly handsome, with sun-streaked brown hair and the warmest dark eyes. He looked older—muscular and manly—at least sixteen! When their eyes first met, Amanda was surprised by the jolt of electricity. She blushed and quickly lowered her head in prayer. She would never boldly look at him, but Sunday after Sunday, she could feel him staring. It raised prickles along the back of her neck.

He always came alone. Someone said he was a deckhand at the Cape Light docks, but lived in the neighboring town of Cranberry. There was a fine house of worship in Cranberry, so why was he coming to her father's church?

"Amanda, over here!" her best friend Kat called. Kat's cousin Lizabeth stood next to her and waved. Amanda hung her shawl on a coat rack and headed toward her friends, past the long table groaning with potato salad, fried fish, fried chicken, cole slaw, baked beans, and a whole ham. The little kids were jostling each other to get to Mrs. White's famous lemon meringue pie.

"Allemande left and allemande right," the fiddler called. Amanda made her way around the lively dancers. There was Father swinging a thrilled, laughing Hannah off her feet. Amanda was happy to see Father giving his full attention to her six-year-old sister; Hannah needed it so much. At least tonight I don't have to take care of her, Amanda thought. I'm free as a bird! She immediately felt guilty. It's not as if I'm kept in a *cage*, she told herself. I'm glad to mother Hannah and keep house for Father. It's the least I can do.

"Do-si-do and stop right there," the fiddler called, "back to the girl with the ribbon in her hair."

"Look at Mr. Witherspoon," Kat said when Amanda reached her friends. Mr. Witherspoon, the baker, fancied himself an expert square dancer and his feet managed extra-intricate steps in spite of the bulk of his body. Near him, Kat's mother and father whirled in graceful circles. Some of their classmates—Mark, Billy, Mabel, and Joanna—danced exuberantly, bumping into each other and laughing.

"Everyone's here," Lizabeth said.

"Well . . . not *everyone*," Amanda said. She bit her lip. She hadn't meant to hint about that boy. Lizabeth always noticed bad things about him. "That one Sunday suit he wears to church? It has shiny worn spots," Lizabeth would say. "All right, he's handsome, but he's nobody, Amanda." Lizabeth could be funny and generous, but she could also be a terrible snob.

"I meant I don't see everyone from our class," Amanda corrected herself.

Lizabeth swept her words aside. "You meant that boy from church, didn't you?"

Amanda shrugged. "I don't think he'll be here."

"Well, he is," Lizabeth said. "Right there!"

Amanda followed her glance. He was standing on the far side of the large barn. Now he was facing their way!

"Don't look over there," Amanda pleaded.

"He's staring at you," Kat said.

"Is he? Don't look, Kat!"

"And . . . he's coming over!" Kat said.

And then he was standing in front of them. Amanda looked at him, looked down, looked at him, looked away. His focus on her, so close up, was too uncomfortable.

Kat broke the awkward silence. "Hello. I'm Kat."

"And I'm Lizabeth."

Amanda felt as though she had forgotten how to speak. "I'm Amanda," came out breathlessly. She tried to smile through frozen lips.

"I know," he said. "Amanda Morgan. I . . . found out."

Heat rose in Amanda's face. She couldn't think of a single word to say.

There was a long pause.

"You must have a name, too," Kat finally said.

"I . . . um . . ." His eyes were glued to Amanda's.

Suddenly everyone else seemed to have become invisible. "Do you think . . . Would you like to dance?"

Amanda nodded.

He led her to the dance floor. Leaving her friends felt like stepping into deep water.

They danced to "Turkey in the Straw" in total silence. He frowned, concentrating on the steps. Amanda, normally a good dancer, felt wooden. A last flourish from the band and it was over.

I was too shy, Amanda thought. He thinks I have no personality. I bored him. He'll say "thank you" and leave.

But when "Arkansas Traveler" started, he led her to another circle. A few steps together, and then he promenaded her in the wrong direction. They danced smack into Mr. Witherspoon! The baker's horrified expression was too comical! The boy laughed sheepishly and Amanda joined in and soon they were both laughing hard, all their nervousness going into it.

"Sorry, Mr. Witherspoon," Amanda gasped.

"Promenade right," Mr. Witherspoon muttered. "*Right*, not left. *Right!*"

"Right, sir," the boy said. That set them off again— they couldn't stop laughing, and they had to leave the dance floor.

"We were just awful," Amanda said. "Poor Mr. Witherspoon takes it all so seriously."

They found two empty spots on a bench past the refreshment table.

"I have a terrible sense of direction." He grinned. "Now if they'd called promenade to starboard . . ."

"You're a seaman?"

"I work on the *Mary Lee*."

"On the Cape Light docks? I know that boat," Amanda said. "It looks trim and shipshape."

He nodded. "Captain Young is a tough boss. Not that I blame him."

"Do you go to school, too, or—"

"No, I quit last spring when I turned sixteen. I liked school all right, but I have other plans. I'm a deckhand here for now, but that's just marking time until I can ship out on a whaler. Out of Nantucket."

"A whaler! That's *dangerous*, isn't it?"

"It's real adventure!" His eyes shone. "My grandpa sailed all over the South Seas on whalers and my oldest brother came back from a two-year voyage a while ago. He came back a *man*. See, working on a boat like the *Mary Lee*—that's almost like factory work. Almost as dull and repetitive as working in a cannery, where my

7

father seems content enough. Not me! I was born for the high seas."

He gazed off into space and Amanda studied his profile—his perfectly straight nose, his intense expression. He could be a finely sculpted figurehead at the prow of a great ship, looking forward over a turbulent sea. It was the most romantic image!

He turned back to her. "Do you know what a Nantucket sleigh ride is?"

"No. I've never heard of that."

"When they get a harpoon into a sperm whale, it'll keep diving, pulling out more and more line. And then it might swim off at tremendous speed, dragging the boat behind it. It's like a gale wind is blowing and the boat flies along the sea surface, leaping from crest to crest of the waves and you hear a bunch of cracks like pistol shots. The spray drenches you and you can't even see the whale. You just hold on. That's what they call a Nantucket sleigh ride. My grandfather told me."

"It sounds thrilling," Amanda said.

"It sure does." His face was lit up with excitement. "Though my grandpa says it's no fun. He's seen a boat, crew, and whale vanish down into the sea, quick as a blink."

"I don't want you to vanish," Amanda said. Somehow talking to him had become easy as anything.

His smile melted her. "I'm aiming to be around."

"I don't know your name yet."

"Jed Langford."

Jed Langford. Of course he'd have a beautiful name!

The band struck up the Virginia reel.

"Ready to give it another try?" he asked.

"Let's, but we should stay out of Mr. Witherspoon's way," Amanda laughed.

Virginia reel. Ladies' Choice. Fox in the Henhouse. They danced and danced, and each time the fiddler's call made them part, it was wonderful to come together again.

Amanda's eyes were shining and her smile was radiant. Another dance and another, whirling; his hand at her waist, swinging; he smelled of soap and lemon, circling, she'd go on forever and ever . . . until the band took a break.

Amanda's dress was sticking to her. Her forehead was damp with perspiration.

"Whew, it's hot in here." Jed rolled up the sleeves of his blue flannel shirt. "Want to get some air?"

"That's just what I need."

Outside they passed a pile of lumber left over from the barn raising. *The single happiest evening of my entire life,* Amanda thought. *But I wish it wasn't happening because the Hallorans' old barn was struck by lightning.*

They found a bale of hay off the path to sit on.

"So tell me all about Amanda Morgan," Jed said.

"There's not much to tell," Amanda said. "I don't know where to start."

"How about at the beginning?"

"Well, let's see. You know my father's the minister. I think he's the finest man in Cape Light. He's truly good and kind. I want you to meet him."

"I'll introduce myself after church tomorrow. You're lucky. I wish I thought that much of *my* father," Jed said.

"You don't?" Amanda asked.

"We fight a lot. He's trying to keep me from shipping out. See, he doesn't have a bit of spirit. He works at the cannery, and it's that new mass production. They call it an assembly line. He does the same little thing all day long. It has to wear him down, but he's afraid to change jobs. So I can't look up to him. On top of that, he does his best to discourage *me*!"

"Oh. I'm sorry. That must be hard for you."

"He's *nothing* like my grandpa. Well, anyway . . . What else, Amanda? What do you like the most?"

"That's easy—I guess being in the church choir is just about my favorite thing. I love to sing: all kinds of songs, when I'm happy or sad or anything."

"I know how that is. I wish I could play a real instrument. Boy, I'd like that more than anything! I have a harmonica that I fool around with. Though I wish I could play the trumpet." He stopped and grinned. "Loud and brassy, like me."

"You're not brassy," Amanda said.

"It was pretty brassy to come over to meet you, right in the middle of your friends. I'm not always that bold—only when something's important to me. Anyway, when the trumpet's played right, it can get the most golden, soulful sound. I heard someone play 'Taps' once in a way that could make grown men cry."

Nothing about his rugged appearance led Amanda to suspect that he'd have a feeling for music, too. But there it was! Could he be more perfect?

"I hear you over all the others in church," Jed said. "When you sing 'Amazing Grace'—I like the way you embroider all over the melody."

Amanda smiled. "I've never heard it called embroidery before. It's such a wonderful, simple melody. It just invites me to go under and above the regular notes and get fancy with it."

Jed nodded. Their eyes met and Amanda thought he *had* to feel their connection, too.

"The choirmaster asked me to do a solo, but I won't."

"You ought to."

"Kat says I should, but I want to enjoy singing without getting nervous about it." The connection to Jed felt so very strong that Amanda began to chatter to cover her confusion. "Kat Williams and Lizabeth Merchant—you just met them—are my best friends. You know that huge white house on Lighthouse Lane, just past the village green? That's where Lizabeth lives. And Kat's father is the lighthouse keeper and we always go to the tower room. It's our special place. And . . . what else? My sister Hannah's six and I take care of her. Well, because . . . because my mother died when Hannah was born."

"I'm sorry," Jed said. "I thought it was something like that. I mean, I never saw a woman in church with you."

"I miss her." Especially now, Amanda thought,

when I want to tell her about Jed. "What brings you to our church?" she asked. "I guess your family worships in Cranberry. Don't you like the minister? Reverend Cranston seems very nice."

"It's nothing like that."

"Then why?"

"Do you want to hear the truth?"

"Well, of course!"

"All right, the truth." He hesitated for a moment. "I was working at the Cape Light docks and I saw you and a red-haired girl—Kat, I guess—walking by. You were the most beautiful girl I'd ever seen."

"Me?" Had he actually said that?

"But you had the saddest eyes. I had to meet you. I wanted to—I don't know—to make you smile."

"I think you just did." He had come to Cape Light every Sunday for *her*! Amanda stared up at the night sky and took a deep breath. Were the stars ever that close before? Did hay ever smell so sweet?

Their words tumbled out, spilling over each other.

Jed had four older brothers and a pet goat. "You'd never think a goat could be that smart and answer to its own name! But it eats everything in sight, chewed up my shirt right off the line!"

"I'd love having a pet," Amanda said. "A puppy, a kitten, anything. I love animals. But no one's at home during the day to take care of it."

Jed's favorite dessert was apple brown Betty. . . . Amanda liked pussy willows, even if they weren't showy. . . . As soon as he had some money saved, Jed was getting a big globe with all the oceans and continents. . . . Amanda loved when the Mill Pond froze over for skating. . . . Jed knew her eyes were hazel, but he saw them turn green when sunlight hit her pew. . . .

Is *this* what falling in love is like? Amanda wondered. Needing to share every detail, being fascinated by the least little thing about him, half breathless with anticipation, filled with a tingling glow. . . . She'd had no idea!

They talked until Amanda shivered in the night chill. "I left my shawl in the barn."

"I wish I had a jacket to give you."

"I think we'd better go inside."

On the path to the barn, Jed took her hand. His felt rough and calloused, the hand of a working man, both strange to her and somehow familiar. They were holding hands! All the magazines said that was improper unless a couple was engaged. Amanda felt guilty, she *knew* better, but she couldn't pull her hand from the warmth of his.

❦ *two* ❦

Sunday morning, October 22, 1905

A manda woke up to a gray Sunday morning, but she felt flooded with sunshine. She stretched slowly and luxuriously. She could still feel Jed's fingerprints on her hand. It had been so wonderful, it could have been a dream—but it wasn't. It was real and happening to *her*!

Jed would be in church today. She'd see him again in an hour—how could an hour seem so *long*! She would introduce him to Father and maybe he could come to lunch after church. . . . Tuna salad. She knew how to make it tasty, with onions and celery. No, not tuna! He might be awfully tired of fish from working on the *Mary Lee*. Egg salad? Deviled eggs?

She heard the rattle of dishes from downstairs. Father and Hannah must be at breakfast already! She rushed to get dressed in her very best Sunday dress, blue—like Jed's shirt!—with a deep ruffle grazing her ankles.

She stopped to look in the mirror over the scratched pine dresser. Kat and Lizabeth often told her she was the prettiest girl in town. Mr. Thomas, the postmaster, had said that once, too. She could never quite grasp it. The mirror showed the same face she'd always seen there. Light brown hair. Pale skin. Just me— Amanda.

But Jed thought she was beautiful. Her hand touched the silver brush-and-comb set that had been her mother's. Today she *felt* beautiful from deep inside.

She found Father and Hannah in the kitchen, finishing their oatmeal.

"Good morning," Amanda sang out. "Sorry I'm late."

"That's all right," Father said. "We managed. There's some warm for you in the pot."

Amanda served herself. Plain oatmeal, without the cinnamon she usually added. Well, Father didn't know. "Sorry, I guess I overslept. After all that dancing."

"I had so much fun!" Hannah said. "Fun, fun, fun!"

Amanda gave her a radiant smile, her happiness spilling over in all directions. She joined them at the table.

"Hannah, if you're finished," Father said, "why don't you wait for us in the yard? Please, we'll be out in a minute."

Amanda was puzzled as she watched Hannah skip out. "But I still have to braid her hair. And I hope she manages to keep her church dress clean. . . ."

"I want to talk to you privately." Father pushed his bowl aside. "I didn't notice last night, with so many people to greet and Hannah—"

"She loved the attention from you."

"But then Mrs. White mentioned it to me," Father continued.

"Mrs. White? Mentioned what?"

"Amanda, you danced every dance with the same boy. All evening long. You shouldn't have done that. It was improper."

Amanda flushed. She moved her spoon back and forth on the wooden surface of the table.

"I know you didn't mean any harm," Father said, "though that boy should have known better than to keep you to himself. You're much too young for anything of that sort."

"His name is Jed Langford and it wasn't his fault at all. I *wanted* to be with him. I like him. Oh, Father, I do like him!" Amanda took a breath and the rest came out in a rush. "He'll be at church this morning and I hope we can invite him for lunch after and—You'll see that he's nice and—"

"Amanda, stop! You're certainly not going to have gentlemen callers at your age. I forbid it."

"Not *callers*," she whispered. "Only one. Only Jed. Just because Mrs. White said—"

"You know I don't worry about what anyone else says. I care about you." Father cleared his throat. "A girl shouldn't be courting until she's close to a marriageable age. At least sixteen, I would think. To avoid a lot of problems. . . ." He kept his eyes on the napkin that he was unconsciously folding and unfolding.

Amanda had never seen Father look so flustered. She wished for any kind of interruption—Hannah running in, a neighbor needing advice, *anything*!

"You understand what I mean, don't you?" Now Father's piercing dark eyes were on her. "You shouldn't be keeping company until you're ready to be engaged."

Amanda nodded. Her joy had vanished as quickly as air rushing out of a punctured balloon.

Father sighed. "It's not easy for me. Your mother would have explained better." He straightened up in his chair. "I trust you to do the right thing, Amanda. You'll politely but firmly discourage him."

"Honestly, courting was the very last thing on my mind. I didn't *mean* to find someone I like so much. I wasn't looking for that to happen." She searched Father's face, pleading. "But it *did* happen and I *do* like him, more than I'll ever like anyone again, and I'm sorry I'm only thirteen, but, please Father, I *have* to keep seeing him and—"

"Has it gone that far already? I forbid you to have any contact with that boy." Father rose from the table. "Enough said. Now hurry and get Hannah ready and let's be on our way." He turned back and spoke more softly. "Amanda, I always have your best interests at heart."

"I know that, Father," Amanda answered. She bent her head and stared, unseeing, at her shoes.

Amanda spotted Jed as soon as she entered the church. His face lit up with the warmest smile. She couldn't return it. She couldn't. There was an empty space on the bench next to him, covered with his coat. He removed it as she headed down the aisle. He'd been saving a place for her!

She took Hannah's hand and walked past him. She

glanced back. Jed was giving her a questioning look. She shook her head slightly and led Hannah to seats at the other side near the front. She willed herself not to look back. She kept busy peeling off her gloves.

Father's eloquent sermon in his rich, deep voice brought murmurs of "yes" and "yes, that's right" from the congregation. Everyone respected and admired him. How could I question Father's wisdom? Amanda thought.

She bowed her head in prayer. Please, God, give me the strength to honor and obey my father. Help me to be worthy of him. . . . She fought to resist turning back to steal a glance at Jed.

After the service, Amanda stood with Father and Hannah on the front steps as he greeted the members of the congregation filing past.

"That was powerful, Reverend," Mr. Thomas, the postmaster, said. "You made me stop and think."

Amanda realized she hadn't taken in a word of the sermon. She had sung the hymns in a fog.

The Hallorans, Mrs. Cornell, the Whites, Lizabeth and the rest of the Merchant family, Kat and her family, Kat saying "let's meet at the tower after lunch," the Masons, the Alveiras . . . and then Jed striding toward them past the last of the stragglers.

"Reverend Morgan, I'm Jed Langford." His wide, inviting smile broke Amanda's heart. He held out his hand.

"Yes, I know." Father shook it reluctantly. "I've seen you here."

"I looked forward to meeting you. I've enjoyed your sermons, sir."

"Have you?" All kindness had left Father's voice.

"Good morning, Jed," Amanda whispered. She didn't know she was gripping Hannah's hand so tightly until Hannah said "Ow!" and squirmed loose.

"Good morning, Amanda." Jed squared his shoulders. "Sir, I'd like your permission to call on your daughter."

"Certainly not. My daughter is thirteen. She does not receive callers."

Jed looked from Reverend Morgan to Amanda and back again. He tried to hold his smile. "But sir, I promise you I'll treat her with the greatest respect and—and care."

Reverend Morgan's stance remained stern, and traces of dismay began to spread over Jed's face.

"My answer is no." Father placed his hand on Amanda's shoulder. "Good day, Mr. Langford. Come, girls."

He led his daughters down the steps, leaving Jed standing stunned at the top.

"Father! You've never made anyone feel unwelcome in our church before," Amanda said. "You've never done that!"

"Perhaps I was harsh," Father said. "Of course everyone, sinner or saint, is welcome in church. But that boy—he looks much older and—"

"He's only sixteen."

"—and he's extremely bold and forward and—"

"He's not. You didn't give him a chance."

"It's my duty to protect you."

They were coming to the end of the path. Hannah was almost walking backward, twisting around to face the church.

"For goodness' sake," Amanda said, "don't stare at him!" Jed must be feeling so humiliated! She couldn't leave him like that.

"He's handsome," Hannah piped up. "Is he a bad man?"

"Hush, Hannah," Father said. "We believe no one is bad through and through. Only misguided."

Jed is *not* bad, or misguided, Amanda thought. I *know* him! She stopped short.

"Come along, Amanda."

"One minute, Father," Amanda begged. "Please. Let me talk to him. Only one minute. To . . . at least to be polite."

Father hesitated. "Very well. You know what to tell him."

Amanda hurried back to Jed. "I'm sorry. I'm so sorry." Tears sprang to her eyes. "Father won't allow me to see you."

Jed nodded. "Will you . . . will you meet me somewhere?"

"No. I can't."

"But do you *want* to? I have to know."

"Yes, I want to," Amanda whispered, "but—"

"Then we'll find a place and—"

"I can't. I can't do that." Amanda glanced back at Father, who was watching and waiting impatiently.

One painful heartbeat went by.

"I'll write you," Jed blurted. "Um . . . near the light-house. You know that cave in the rocks? I'll leave a message."

"Amanda!" Father called.

"I have to go," she said.

"Wait—Amanda—I'll look for your answer."

three

"A secret love letter in a cave!" Lizabeth said. "Just like in a novel!"

"He wouldn't send a *love* letter," Amanda said. "He said *message*. Anyway, he didn't say when he'd leave it. There might be nothing there at all."

Amanda, Kat, and Lizabeth were heading for the lighthouse after school. They cut across the village green from William McKinley Road.

At four o'clock in the afternoon, the square at the center of Cape Light was full of activity. The Halloran children were screaming and whooping as they played tag around the statue of the lost fisherman, while Mrs. Halloran tried to rein them in. The milkman's horse and wagon, finished with its rounds, clip-clopped toward Hayward's Livery Stable. The elderly Peabody sisters left the general store, trying to balance their parasols and mesh bags of groceries. *Click-click-click* came from Joe

Hardy's telegraph office as the girls went by. They passed the barbershop with its red-and-white pole, and the bakery.

"It smells like Mr. Witherspoon made something chocolaty," Lizabeth said. "Want to stop in?"

"No, come on, let's get to the lighthouse," Amanda said.

"You're in a real big hurry for just a little 'message,'" Lizabeth teased.

"Kat's mother is sure to have muffins for us," Amanda said. "Anyway, I can't face Mr. Witherspoon just yet."

"Why?" Kat asked.

"I told you, Jed and I couldn't help laughing right in front of him." Amanda smiled at the memory. "We were terrible, but I had the best time of my whole life!"

"Really? Of your *whole* life?" Kat grinned. "Well then, let's hurry to the cave and find his message."

They reached Lighthouse Lane, the long road that ran all along the skinny peninsula jutting into the Atlantic. They rushed past Lizabeth's big house near the green. Here the lane was paved and tall trees with crimson and yellow leaves arched overhead.

"You're the first one of us to fall in love," Kat teased.

"I'm not—I mean, I couldn't be!" Amanda's blush gave her away.

Lizabeth frowned. "You're not taking him *seriously*, are you? He's a deckhand, Amanda. And obviously dirt-poor. And he's not even in school anymore."

"I don't care! I don't care about any of that!" Most of the time Amanda ignored Lizabeth's snobbishness, but now she was truly angry.

"Sorry. Don't get mad at me." Lizabeth studied Amanda curiously. "For goodness' sake, you hardly know him."

The girls trudged on. They passed Amanda's cottage overlooking the shore on the unpaved section of Lighthouse Lane. They could hear the waves crashing against the rocks below the parsonage.

"Half a mile to go," Lizabeth groaned.

"It's not that far." Kat skipped along and her schoolbooks, held together by a leather strap, swung in a wide arc.

Lizabeth is right, Amanda thought, I hardly know him. If I had a bit of sense, I wouldn't be rushing to defy Father for a secret letter.

They came to the steep hill where Lighthouse Lane led down to Wharf Way and the docks. They passed fishermen's cottages. Nets were spread out to dry on some of the porches. Here the lane was lined by dense brush, sea grass, and beach plum.

Lizabeth and Kat were talking about their arithmetic homework.

"Four pages," Kat complained. "Miss Cotter thinks we have nothing else to do."

"I don't mind arithmetic." Lizabeth shrugged. "And I don't have anything else to do."

"Well, *other* people have chores," Kat reminded her.

They passed the bait-and-tackle shed, the rowboat rental sign, and the Alveira and Sons boatyard.

Lizabeth turned to Amanda. "You're awfully quiet. Are you still mad at me?"

"No, of course not," Amanda said. "I'm thinking."

Finally they reached the lighthouse, with its bright red-and-yellow stripes on the side, a clearly visible daytime landmark for sailors.

Below the lighthouse at Durham Point, a small strip of beach was surrounded by huge jagged, black rocks that continued into the sea. A few steps past the tower, rocks on the ocean side of Lighthouse Lane formed a cave.

Amanda, Kat, and Lizabeth stood at its dark mouth.

"Well, go ahead." Lizabeth gave Amanda a little push. "Go on in."

"Maybe I—" Amanda scrunched up her shoulders. "No. No, I changed my mind."

"Wait—what happened?" Kat looked puzzled.

"Aren't you curious to see what Jed wrote?" Lizabeth asked.

Amanda nodded miserably. "But I'm disobeying Father."

"Your father didn't say anything about writing, did he? That's not the same as *seeing* Jed," Kat said.

"I'd still be going against his wishes." But would it hurt to take one quick look, Amanda thought. Just to see if Jed had left a letter? "Maybe I'm starting something— something that I shouldn't. That I won't know how to finish."

"You don't have to answer if you don't want to," Kat said.

"This *is* romantic," Lizabeth said. "Even if I don't quite approve."

Amanda shifted from one leg to the other.

"Well, make up your mind," Kat said. "We're not going to stand here all day, are we?"

"Come inside with me." Amanda tugged at Kat's hand.

"You're not *scared*, are you?" Kat asked.

Amanda shrugged. "Not of the cave."

"It's awfully dark," Lizabeth said, peering into the black opening. "There could be bats. Why couldn't Jed pick a nicer place to leave a letter?"

"Because it has to be hidden, and anyway, he's making it easy for me. I told him I come to the lighthouse a lot," Amanda said.

"Should I run to the cottage and get a hurricane lamp?" Kat said.

"I don't think he'd leave it deep inside, do you?" Amanda said. "Let's look near the entrance first."

"At least it's dry," Lizabeth said as she followed Kat and Amanda into the cave. "I'm wearing new shoes."

Amanda scanned the dark stone walls. Generations of Cape Light youngsters had used the cave to play hide-and-seek or to scare themselves half to death with ghost stories.

"Here's something!" Kat said. "Look." She took a brown paper bag from a crevice, about six steps in from the entrance on the left side of the cave.

Amanda reached inside and pulled out a piece of lined notepaper.

"A paper bag," Lizabeth sniffed. "In a novel it would

29

be engraved Crane's stationery from Boston. With a personal wax seal. Honestly, he—"

"Jed did the smart thing," Amanda interrupted. "A stationery envelope would show up too much—children do come in here sometimes, you know." She had to defend him to Lizabeth, though she was dismayed by the crumpled bag.

"Hmmm . . . Well *maybe* that's why," Lizabeth said. "Aren't you going to read it?" she prodded.

Amanda's hands shook as she unfolded the piece of notepaper.

Dear Amanda,
    What should I do to change your father's mind? Please write back.

                      Yours, Jed

It was so disappointing! Amanda had to close her eyes to picture Jed's handsome face and square shoulders and remember why she liked him.

"Come on, read it out loud!" Lizabeth said.

Amanda shook her head. The stiff sentence and the poor penmanship embarrassed her.

"She doesn't have to," Kat said. "It's personal."

"Well, is it a love letter?" Lizabeth asked.

"Not exactly."

That evening, Amanda took her pretty pink stationery out of the drawer. It was her best set, a birthday gift, and she had been saving it. She put a drop of her violet toilet water on a piece of cotton and rubbed it on a corner of a page. She sniffed critically. Was the smell too obvious? Maybe she should start another page—but she hated to waste one. All that time waiting between the rocks of a cave, she thought, will air it out. And she did want Jed to have a faint whiff, just enough to remind him of her at the barn dance, the way she couldn't forget his soap-and-lemon smell.

October 30, 1905
Dear Jed,

I found your letter in the cave. There isn't anything you can do to change Father's mind. When he is sure he's right, nothing can budge him. You didn't do or say anything wrong. You were perfect.

I go the lighthouse to be with my friends mostly on Tuesdays because that's when Hannah plays at her friend Mary Margaret's house. Sometimes I have a free afternoon in between. Anyway, I'll look for your letters and leave mine for you mostly on Tuesdays.

I know I shouldn't do this, but the barn dance was the very best evening of my life and I can't think about anything but you.

Love, Amanda

Amanda reread her words. She'd been carried away in that last paragraph. It was far too forward! She couldn't possibly send it and she'd wasted a page of good stationery! She dabbed a bit of toilet water on a fresh one. She rewrote the first two paragraphs and left out the last one. And she signed it "Sincerely, Amanda." Now it sounded stiff and self-conscious, but she *felt* stiff and self-conscious; it was the best she could do.

November 7, 1905
Dear Amanda,

I'm far from perfect, but thanks for saying I didn't do nothing wrong. Your letter smells like you and makes me wish to see you even more. Tuesdays are going to be my lucky day. As for

perfect—I have a quick temper and I get into
fistfights when someone crosses me, though I try
to be peaceable, and my Ma says I forget to put
things away and leave them all over the place.
Perfect is you.

Yours, Jed

This letter was so much better than his first one, Amanda thought. This sounded more like Jed talking to her at the barn dance. It didn't matter one bit that it came in a paper bag. "Perfect is you." Oh, my! Who cared if that was written on rough notepaper?

As the messages flew back and forth in the cave, Amanda began to feel as though she was opening her heart to a diary—a living, breathing diary that cared. And as Jed began to do the same, he seemed eloquent to her. Strange how you can put things down in writing, Amanda thought, that you would never dare say face to face. Maybe Jed and I know each other far better this way than we ever would from courting in the front parlor.

November 25, 1905
Dear Jed,
I read your letters over and over. I know I

should destroy them to be safe, but I can't make myself do it. I tied them with a ribbon, forget-me-not blue for remembrance, and keep them at the bottom of my glove drawer. I know it is hard to see each other only across the aisle in church, but I can't do as you ask and meet you. I won't be a sneak. I respect my father too much. I think you are brave to keep coming to our church. I hope you have a nice Thanksgiving.

Your Amanda

On a raw, gray day at the end of November, Amanda and Hannah were leaving the post office with a handful of mail for Father. They had just stepped onto East Street. At the same moment, Jed came out of the carriage repair shop nearby. Amanda stopped short so abruptly that Hannah asked, "What's wrong?"

"Hello," Jed said.

"Hello," Amanda said. She had to catch her breath. "You know my little sister, Hannah."

Hannah stared up at him.

Jed and Amanda stood still, transfixed, taking each other in. The wind whipped Amanda's hair around and bit at her face.

"Let's go. I'm *freezing*," Hannah finally said. "It's *cold*!"

"Can we go somewhere?" Jed looked around frantically. "Somewhere indoors?"

Amanda bit her lip. "I wish . . . I can't."

Mrs. Peabody passed by. "Hello there, Amanda. Don't keep your little sister out in this cold, dear. It's frostbite weather."

"Hello, Mrs. Peabody. I won't. We're just going home."

Mrs. Peabody continued on her way, but she glanced back for a curious look at Jed.

"Come on, Amanda," Jed urged.

"I'm sorry, I can't," Amanda whispered. It was all she could do to take Hannah's hand and continue on down East Street.

November 28, 1905
Dear Jed,

    It made me sad to leave you on the street this afternoon. Cape Light is such a small town and we're bound to run into each other. But everyone knows me and my father, and yesterday there was Hannah, too, and she listens to everything. Cape Light is a very special place because people care about each other and help each other. You can always count on your neighbors. But the bad side of it is that everyone knows everyone else's business. Especially mine, because I'm the minister's daughter and somehow that makes everything I do more public. I'm afraid to get anyone talking about us. It was good to see you, even for a minute, and I hope we run into each other again, but we have to be satisfied with just saying hello. For now, anyway.

I hope my father will bend a little, perhaps when I'm fifteen—I'm sure he said fifteen, not sixteen, once. Even fifteen is almost two years away and a long time to wait. I know that's a lot to ask of you.

I'm saving up loads of things to show you. We have a Berliner Gramophone and a cylinder of Enrico Caruso singing. I want to listen to it with you in the parlor when you can finally come calling. It's scratchy, but his voice is so beautiful that you forget about the scratches. He sings in Italian, so I don't understand a word but I understand the emotion. Have you ever

*heard music that makes you want to laugh and
celebrate and cry real tears all at the same time?
Does that sound too crazy?*

Your Amanda

December 1, 1905
Dear Amanda,
     *It was hard to run into you and then have
you leave so fast. It seems to me you care too much
about what other people think. I'm hoping you'll
change your mind about meeting me somewhere.*
     *I had a dream about you last night. You
were wearing that same gray skirt and jacket
that you wore to church last Sunday. You kissed
my cheek, light as a whisper, and I woke up
missing you so bad.*

Amanda felt the heat rise in her cheeks. He mustn't
dream of her that way! Was he too bold, as Father said?
It took a moment before her delicious confusion allowed
her to continue reading.

*What you said about music making you sad
and happy and sometimes both all at once doesn't*

37

*sound crazy to me. Music gets to me, too.
Remember the Spanish-American War back in
1898? I guess you were too young. I was nine.
When they played those John Philip Sousa
marches like "The Stars and Stripes Forever" and
the march from El Capitan, and most of all, the
Rough Riders' favorite, "Hot Time in the Old
Town Tonight," well, I wanted to march off that
minute and join the Rough Riders Cavalry! Me
and my friends played Rough Riders all the time
and we fought over who could be Colonel
Roosevelt. That was before he became president.*

*The next year, there was a small ceremony
when Cranberry updated the plaque in front of
the Town Hall. Did you ever notice it? It lists all
the men from Cranberry and the towns around
here who were killed in war, all the way back to
the Revolution. Some men from the Civil War
days came. Some of them were missing legs or
arms. There was only one man from around here
killed in the Spanish-American War: Daniel
Cornell from Cape Light. Do you know his
people? I don't know if he was in the Rough
Riders or not. If the music for it wasn't so good, I*

bet a lot less men would go marching off to war.

At the ceremony, a man named William Granville played "Taps" on the trumpet and he bent and twisted the notes in a way I'd never heard it before. Like you said, it made me want to cry real tears and at the same time celebrate that something could sound so beautiful. Then I did a real stupid thing. Listen, I was only ten. I went to William Granville's house. I asked him if he'd give me trumpet lessons. Well, he looked me up and down and asked what I planned to use for a trumpet and I had no answer for that. And then he asked what made me think he'd want to be bothered with me? I hate William Granville still. Ma says that I'm way too proud and that I hold grudges forever when someone cuts me down to size.

I never told anyone about William Granville before. I have lots of friends in Cranberry, on my street and from when I went to school, but we mostly play ball and horse around and don't talk about private stuff. Not the way I do with you.

So about waiting for you for that terrible long time. You're the prettiest girl I ever did see *but it's about a lot more than prettiness.*

If I ever get my father to sign permission for me to ship out, a whaling voyage can take 2 or 3 years. See, the waters around New England are pretty much fished out, so whalers have to travel far, to the South Seas and beyond. That's why it takes so long. Will you wait for me, too?

Love, Jed

December 5, 1905
Dear Jed,

Yes, I'll wait for you. How soon would you go? If whaling is your passion, I guess you have to follow it. I don't have a goal of my own. Kat Williams has the goal of being an artist and I admire her talent and determination so much. I wish I had something special of my own. But then I think I do have something special, and that's writing to you!

I'm glad you told me about William Granville. You did nothing to be ashamed of. He was awful. What my father always says is, before you decide to hate someone for being mean, you have to stop and think that you don't know what's going on in his life right then. Maybe he had a dreadful fight with his wife just before you knocked on his door, or he just learned he had tuberculosis.

Daniel Cornell's widow is Mrs. Cornell from the Pelican Book Shop. She goes to our church and I know her from the bookstore. I like to read, but I don't go into the store often. Lizabeth has an account there and she buys the new books and passes them around to the rest of us. I know Mrs. Cornell just to say hello, how are you. I was very little when her husband was killed and I don't remember much about it.

I think about you all the time. Sometimes I even think I smell your lemon skin tonic that I liked so much.

Love, Amanda

December 15, 1905
My beautiful Amanda,

I'm hopping mad! If I didn't have you to write to, I'd be punching walls and breaking things. I just had another big fight with my father. I need him to sign the permission because

I'm under 18 and he's stalling. Says whaling is a dying industry. Everything has its ups and downs, doesn't it? I bet whalebone corsets come back in style. And whale oil for lamps. With all his old-woman worrying and stick-in-the-mud ways, he's breaking a proud family tradition. I have no patience for him. I'm lucky I have my grandpa.

It's not all for the adventure of it either, though I was born for the high seas like I told you. There's good money in whaling, or there used to be. And I'm betting there will be again. Back in 1882, sperm oil was $1.06 a gallon and last year it was down to 31 cents. Grandpa says it stands to reason that it's bottomed out and has to go up again any time now. It's the only way I know to make a pile of money to offer you nice things. I'd come back to you with lace and silks, and perfumes from Araby.

I'm not sure when I can ship out. I heard there's no whalers out of Nantucket anymore and only a handful sailing out of New Bedford, a sorry state, though I hear they're looking for crew that's not vagabonds and runaways. There's whalers sailing out of San Francisco, but that's an awful long way for me to get there.

I don't have aftershave tonic. I rubbed a cut lemon all over myself that night so I wouldn't smell fishy.

Love, Jed

Amanda colored. There was something much too intimate about picturing him rubbing a lemon all over. And Lizabeth would have a lot to say about fish odors if she knew! Amanda quickly brushed that out of her mind and wrote:

I don't care about lace, silks, and perfumes.

The pile of letters began to overflow her glove drawer. She started a new packet with another ribbon.

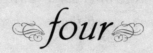

four

In church Amanda sat in the front row with Hannah. Sunday after Sunday, she had to resist turning to look back at Jed. As it was, Father kept a watchful eye on her and had a frown for Jed. But when she rose to sing with the choir, she faced the congregation—and Jed.

"Amazing grace," she sang, "how sweet the sound . . ." Love is a kind of grace, Amanda thought, isn't it? "I once was lost but now I am found . . ."

Jed's eyes burned into hers. The air between them was thick with the words exchanged in their letters.

April 23, 1906
Dear Jed,

You looked sad and tired in church yesterday. And so handsome that I almost gasped in front of everyone! Did you have another fight with your father? I'll tell Kat to ask her father if it looks like whaling will come back. I think he'd know. He used to work on a whaler until he hurt his leg in an accident at sea and became the lighthouse keeper.

I told you about the new girl, Rose Forbes, who moved on to Lighthouse Lane right across from me in March. She's more quiet than Kat and Lizabeth, but interesting—she's from New York City! We've become very good friends. Mrs. Forbes is a great beauty. You must have noticed her in church.

Rose has the same coloring as Mrs. Forbes— ivory skin and black hair and eyes. You've probably seen her in church, too. Rose isn't as strikingly beautiful as her mother, but she has a beautiful heart. I want you two to meet. She's very kind and sensitive to other people's feelings. I help Rose take care of her horse, Midnight Star, at Clayton Stables whenever I have time. He's difficult because he was abused. Rose convinced her Uncle Ned—he owns Clayton's—to keep him until the horse fair in North Menasha. Anyway, now there are four of us—me, Kat, Lizabeth, and

Rose—who go up to the tower and talk for hours.

We're all shocked by the San Francisco earthquake—we didn't get the news here for days after April 18th. Now that terrible fire seems to be going on and on to destroy the whole city. The newspaper says there are at least 700 dead and probably more. I had a nightmare about it. I keep thinking there's a harsh world outside Cape Light where a beautiful horse like Midnight Star gets abused and helpless people are caught in an earthquake. The only thing I can do is pray for all of them. I wish I could do more. I'm grateful to live in a place that is peaceable and good and kind. I hope Cape Light never changes.

Love, Amanda

April 30, 1906
Dear Jed,

The most surprising thing happened at the East Menasha horse fair last Saturday. Rose had been practicing jumps with Midnight Star because she wanted to save him by showing off his abilities. You know the riding events are for boys and men only. Well, Rose was going to

*disguise herself as a boy! Then at the last
minute, she decided she'd do better if she rode
Midnight Star as herself. In front of all those
people! And wearing a divided skirt because she
had to ride astride to give Midnight Star the
proper signals! I wish you could have seen her—
she and Star were magnificent. I'm in awe of her
bravery. A lot of people were shocked and there'll
be gossip for months. But Rose held her head up
high and didn't care. She says she did it because
of her love for Midnight Star. It's wonderful to do
what you feel is right, no matter what anyone
thinks. I hope I'll be as brave if I'm ever tested.*

*Rose's mother invited me, Father, and
Hannah to dinner last night. Their house has
changed entirely since old Mr. Reynolds lived
there. The dining room is pale yellow and mostly
bare, with none of the mementos and collections
you see everywhere else. It's airy and pretty,
though certainly different. Our house seemed
gloomy and cluttered when we came home.*

*Anyway, there were the Forbeses, Mrs.
Cornell, the Claytons, and the Haverstraws. I
hadn't seen Father so relaxed and cheerful in a*

long time. He was giving extra attention to Mrs.
Cornell. Of course Father knows Mrs. Cornell
from church and from browsing in her bookstore.
He likes history and she has a good collection
of books about the early days right here in
Massachusetts. But this was the first time we've
seen her socially. She seemed to make him really
laugh, and not just politely, though I didn't think
she said anything that witty. I'm sure you've
heard that he visits parishioners, to counsel and
comfort, at all hours of the day and night. It's
because he's such a kind man, of course, but I
also think he threw himself into too many good
works to bury his grief about losing Mama. And
then maybe he got used to everyone needing him,
so he never stopped. Anyway, I suppose it's good
that he is laughing again.

    Do I sound like a terrible person if I resent
that it's Mrs. Cornell, a stranger, who can make
him happy instead of me and Hannah? I do
sound terrible! I'm glad he had a pleasant
evening out and delicious roast duckling with
orange sauce that I certainly can't make. Well,
Mrs. Forbes told me she can't either; it was

prepared by their cook, Edna.

Please don't think that I'm criticizing Father. He is a wonderful man. I wish he would give you a chance to find that out.

Love, Amanda

May 4, 1906
Dear Amanda,

If you want to do what's right no matter what anyone thinks, then be brave enough to meet me! Or at least spend some time with me when we run into each other by accident, no matter who is looking. If you ask me, it's not right to pretend like we hardly know each other, like yesterday when you were coming down North Street. I wish you'd be brave about it like your friend Rose.

I won't say nothing against your father, though he sure hasn't shown me his best side. But it's wrong for him to neglect you that way. It bothers me you have to do housework and cooking and watch your sister all the time. I want to tuck you in my shirt pocket and take care of you. . . .

May 13, 1906
Dear Jed,

    Rose's bravery about doing what she thinks is right is not the same thing at all. She wasn't defying someone she loves. You're asking me to choose between you and my father. Please don't do that. It would break my heart.

    I was surprised to see you in church this morning. You saw how empty it was. People are afraid to be in crowds because of the scarlet fever. Our school closed early and the Strawberry Festival was canceled. So many people I know are sick, friends from school and Lizabeth's little sister, Tracy. She's only four—it's awful! I've been praying for her and for everyone else. Maybe you shouldn't come to Cape Light until it's over. Though I'd miss seeing you like anything. When we talked on the church steps this morning, even though it was just for that second, Father noticed and had words with me about it. But it was worth it to hear your voice!

                     Love, Amanda

May 17, 1906
Dear Amanda,

Nothing would keep me from church—not scarlet fever, or hurricanes, or earthquakes, or even your father's nasty looks. I can't go without seeing you, even from a distance. I'm sorry your friend's sister is sick. I think most people get better from scarlet fever, but don't take any chances. Don't let anyone with the sickness breathe on you. That's what they say spreads it. . . .

June 5, 1906
Dear Jed,

I couldn't write and I didn't go to the lighthouse for a while. I just wanted to cry and cry. Lizabeth's little sister Tracy died on May 18th. Rose and Kat, too, are trying to comfort Lizabeth, but I understand how she feels more than anyone. Lizabeth and I have drawn closer than we ever were before. Tracy was so sunny. I always thought she was extra-bright for a four-year-old. She had beautiful dark blue eyes. She used to call me Amanda Jane because she was proud she knew my middle name. Father tells me to pray for acceptance of the things I don't understand, and I do. But I can't help asking: How could God take little Tracy? And why my mother?

Sharing Lizabeth's grief stirs up the pain for my mother as raw and fresh as if it was yesterday. I was seven and all excited about getting a new baby. I saw the carriages in front of our house when I came home from school that afternoon—the midwife's carriage and Dr. Clark from Cranberry, we didn't have a doctor in Cape Light then—and I ran in the front door and heard a baby squalling. I was so excited, but then some grown-ups held me back from going upstairs and I saw Father crying and someone turned me around fast, but I saw the midwife bringing bloody towels down the stairs. I was hustled to a neighbor's house, no one told me anything, and I was so scared. Jed, I never got to say good-bye.

After Mama died, a maiden aunt of Father's came to Cape Light to take care of me and newborn Hannah. You could tell Great-aunt Myrtle was just doing her duty and didn't want to be there. I spent every minute I could at Kat's.

The Williamses practically adopted me and I love them like my own family. It was a relief when Great-aunt Myrtle left.

The terrible thing is that I can't remember Mama's face. It's blurred in my mind. We have a small portrait of her that was painted by one of those traveling artists passing through Cape Light. I don't know if it's a good likeness. And anyway it's only that one moment, that one expression. I try so hard to recall Mama's face. I remember long, dark hair falling over me when she kissed me good night, and a soft hand on my cheek, and the fragrance of violets. That's the cologne I use, too. I remember a golden glow surrounding me, her love warming me like sunshine. Poor Hannah doesn't have anything to remember. I want to make it up to her in every way I can. Except for her much lighter hair, Hannah resembles Mama's portrait. Sometimes I think Father's pain makes him turn away from Hannah more than he means to.

It's been a bad time for everyone and I'm burdening you with my sadness. No one wants to be around someone who is so weepy. I'm sorry, somehow I've written it all down for you.

Love, Amanda

June 10, 1906
Dear Amanda,
    Don't you ever be sorry about anything you write to me. You can tell me anything. . . .

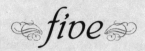

five

Amanda knew her friends were waiting for her at the lighthouse tower. The girl who came for the laundry was late and that made Amanda late. She ran most of the way along Lighthouse Lane—but when she came to the cave, she stopped abruptly. It would take only one minute. . . . Once again, she was full of tingly anticipation. Those crumpled paper bags had become mixed up with the salty air of the ocean, the deep mossy smell of the cave and the crash of the waves against the nearby rocks—the scents and sounds woven around the spell of his letters.

She stepped into the darkness of the cave. There was nothing at all in the crevice. She'd left a letter last Tuesday. More than a week had gone by; Jed had plenty of time to answer. Could he have changed the hiding place? Amanda explored the walls of the cave. She ran her hands over the mossy rocks. Nothing. More than a week and nothing at all.

She trudged up the stairs to the tower. She couldn't hide her disappointment from Kat, Lizabeth, and Rose.

"Amanda, what's wrong?" Rose asked.

"Nothing," Amanda mumbled.

"Well, I have something that'll cheer you right up," Kat said. She waved a brown paper bag.

"Oh!"

"Here," Kat said as she handed it over. "Remember that downpour yesterday? The wind was driving the rain into the cave, so I thought I'd check for a note and save it from getting soaked."

"Thanks!"

"I didn't read it. I didn't open the bag or anything," Kat said.

"I know you didn't." Amanda gave Kat a radiant smile. "Thank you! You saved my life!"

"Is *that* why you looked so sad?" Lizabeth asked. "Just because of one little note?"

"I thought . . . maybe he's losing interest." Amanda fiddled with the crocheted edge of her sleeve. "How can I expect him to keep on writing and waiting and . . . with no hope of spending time with me? Sooner or later, he's going to lose patience."

"He hasn't so far. His letters keep on coming, don't they?" Lizabeth said. "Are you *ever* going to read one to us?"

"No, I'm sorry," Amanda mumbled. She felt uncomfortable. They were her best friends and she would share anything about *herself*, she thought, but she couldn't share Jed's confidences. "I'm sorry, I—I just can't." She tucked the note safely into her dress pocket. She couldn't wait to go home to read it.

"Oh, come on," Lizabeth coaxed. "Just a line or two? We want to hear an honest-to-goodness *love* letter!"

Kat giggled. "Does he write 'Oh my dearest darling, your teeth are just like pearls—they hang by a thread'?"

Lizabeth posed dramatically against the windowsill, her hand to her forehead. "Oh my lovely sweetheart, you are the full moon in the sky of my brain."

Rose laughed. "The sky of your *brain*?"

"I love you madly," Lizabeth went on. "Your eyes are so beautiful, they can't stop looking at each other."

"No, wait," Kat interrupted, "your eyes are like stars, they come out at night."

"I want to kiss-kiss-kiss your hand and your dainty little foot," Lizabeth continued.

Amanda laughed, but she felt the heat rising in her

face. "He doesn't write anything like that."

"Come on, leave her alone," Rose said.

Kat smiled. "But she's so teasable. Look at her blush."

"Aren't you going to share a tiny bit with us?" Lizabeth asked.

"No," Amanda said.

"I guess we'll have to wait to get love letters of our own," Kat said. "Whenever *that* will be!"

"They're not all love letters," Amanda said. "They're about all sorts of things. About his family and his hopes. . . . I do want him to keep on writing!"

Kat looked closely at Amanda. "Has he become that important to you?"

Amanda nodded. "Someday he'll stop, won't he? I have to be prepared for that. Why can't we be *normal*, just seeing each other—" She turned to Rose. "Like you and Chris." Rose and Christopher Merchant, Lizabeth's older brother, had become a couple. "When you and Chris began courting, was it all right with your parents from the beginning?"

"I don't know if Chris and I ever started officially courting," Rose said. "After the horse fair—I guess he was interested in Midnight Star's jumping—he started dropping in at Clayton Stables."

"I happen to know he was interested in a lot more than Midnight Star," Lizabeth put in.

"He began riding and he took to it. And sometimes I'd be mucking out Star's stall and he'd help and we'd talk." Rose smiled. "Lizabeth thought it was terrible that I let him see me shoveling."

"You can't blame me!" Lizabeth said. "It was the *strangest* way of flirting I ever heard of."

"Rose wouldn't know how to flirt if her life depended on it," Amanda said with a smile. Rose didn't know how to be anything but her straightforward self.

"It was relaxed and easy, without the calling cards and the phony manners and all that," Rose said. "We're honestly like best friends."

"I think it could be like that for me and Jed," Amanda said. "If we had half a chance. But I'm afraid of losing him."

"Maybe you could meet him somewhere," Rose said. "Maybe just once or twice?"

"Behind my father's back? I've thought about it. I have. But Father trusts me and I can't betray him. It would feel too awful. I can't do it."

Kat nodded sympathetically. "I know, I couldn't either. I mean, if it was my father. But remember *Romeo and Juliet* last term? There'd be no great love story if Juliet had obeyed *her* father!"

"Being kept apart because of a stupid, old family feud—the Montagues and the Capulets!" Rose said. "See, that's one case where the fathers didn't make much sense."

"And poor Romeo and Juliet had to die instead of living happily ever after," Lizabeth said. "It was all their fathers' fault."

"Maybe—maybe sometimes you're too obedient, Amanda," Rose said.

"No. What do you mean?" Amanda asked.

"Well, you never complain to your father and you never argue," Rose said. She hesitated before she went on. "People can love their parents and still disagree with them. We're a new generation, after all, and going into modern times. Maybe you try *too* hard to please him."

"I want him to be proud of me and I want to set a good example for Hannah," Amanda said. "What's wrong with that? And he's wise. He knows far more than I do about the world."

"But the whole idea of keeping you from Jed—I think that's insulting," Rose said. "He should have enough faith in you—he should know that you would act properly."

Amanda stared at Rose. She had never thought of it that way. She had never questioned the reasons behind Father's rules.

"I'm sorry," Rose said. "I don't mean to be disrespectful. He's a wonderful minister."

"Everyone respects Reverend Morgan," Kat put in. "*Everyone.*"

"I know." Rose cleared her throat. "It's just, well, in the case of Jed, he's acting as a father, not a minister, and he *can* be wrong. You could stand up to him, you know."

Rose doesn't understand, Amanda thought. It's different in a normal family. But in mine, where there's been so much grief, I *have* to be a more dutiful daughter than anyone else! Don't I? Whenever she felt stirrings of rebellion—and that was more often than she wanted to admit—she did her best to squash them.

Amanda gazed out of the tower's window. The sea was deep blue and peaceful today, barely kissing the rocks that lined the strip of beach. The sun was low in the sky, peeking behind drifting clouds of pink and gray. Dear God, Amanda thought, help me to find enough joy in this beautiful world spread before me. Help me to stop longing for what I cannot have.

Lizabeth picked up the binoculars on the windowsill and lazily scanned the horizon. "That's odd," she said.

"What?" Rose asked.

"The sea is perfectly calm. But there's one spot where there's a stream of water shooting up into the air. And something that sort of looks like a rock. . . ."

"Let me see." Kat took the binoculars. "That *is* odd. I think that's whales blowing."

"Whales *blowing*?" Amanda asked. She didn't know the first thing about them.

"Here, look." Kat handed over the binoculars to Amanda. "They spout and the water spews up like that. I'm surprised they're near this coast. Pa says there used to be loads, but they've been pretty much killed off here. That *must* be a pod of whales."

Amanda squinted through the glass. "A *pod*? I thought fish swam in *schools*."

"Whales aren't fish exactly. They're mammals. They nurse and care for their young. Though I don't know why it's called a pod." Kat giggled. "They're a bit larger than *peas*!"

"Jed is going to ship out one day. Soon, I think." Amanda handed the binoculars to Rose.

"My father says whaling isn't what it used to be," Kat said. "He says it's dying."

"Jed's grandfather tells him it's sure to come back," Amanda said.

"I know who his grandfather is. He's very old, but he's still handsome." Kat grinned. "I guess good looks run in that family."

"Jed has his heart set on whaling. I wish I could spend time with him before he goes. Even a little."

"You know what? I bet my mother could change your father's mind," Rose said. "She's very persuasive. When your family comes over for dinner Thursday night—it'll be just us, just family—do you want her to bring up the subject of courtship? Mother loves bringing the right couple together. I could ask her to—"

"No, don't! Please don't! Nothing changes Father's mind when he's sure he's right. And he'll be furious if he thinks I've been complaining to everyone."

Rose's earlier words hammered at Amanda: Father doesn't trust me to behave properly with a boy! But with all I do in the house and all I do for Hannah, I deserve his faith in my good judgment. Amanda did her best to brush away the thoughts and the resentment that came with them.

❧six❧

"This is what I love about summer," Kat said. "Blueberries."

"This is what I hate about summer." Lizabeth slapped her arm. "Mosquitoes."

"Hannah, you're eating the berries faster than you're picking," Amanda said.

"So is Kat." Hannah's grin was surrounded by blue juice.

"All right, we'll both stop now," Kat said.

"Only *three* more?" Hannah asked.

"Come on, Hannah," Rose said. "Kat's mother won't have enough to make a pie for us."

"Two and a half?" Hannah bargained.

The girls laughed. They were kneeling among the wild blueberry bushes near Potter's Orchard.

"Is Hannah's Fourth of July costume all set for tomorrow?" Lizabeth asked Amanda. "If you need help, remember, I have a sewing machine. A treadle is easy to use and it's a million times faster than sewing by hand."

"Thanks," Amanda said, "but it's a simple costume. I don't need to make seams, I'll just belt it and—"

"It's not a *costume*," Hannah complained. "It's only a white sheet with a hole in the middle! The exact same as when I was a ghost for Hallowe'en."

"It's fine. You're one of the white stripes and Miss Cotter suggested a sheet." A branch scratched Amanda's hand as she grabbed for a big bunch of berries.

"I wanted to be Betsy Ross," Hannah said, "and make the flag and have words to say. Miss Cotter is mean!"

"No, she's not," Amanda said. "It's awfully nice of her to direct the Fourth of July pageant."

Hannah shrugged and popped another berry into her mouth. "The stripes march and sing 'Yankee Doodle Dandy.' I like that."

"I can't wait to see you," Rose said. The children's pageant was the cutest event of the Fourth of July celebrations at the town square.

Hannah brightened. "Miss Cotter said even the white stripes can have something special on our heads. As long as it's red, white, and blue."

"You mean ribbons?" Lizabeth asked. "I have plenty to give you."

"Mary Margaret and Belinda and Gwendolyn are going to have hair ribbons. I bet all the girls will! I want something *special*." She looked at Amanda. "Can I wear a big red-white-and-blue hat?"

Amanda sighed. "We don't have a red-white-and-blue hat. Big or small."

"Please, please?" Hannah begged.

"Where in the world would I get one?" Amanda asked.

"I'll bring my ribbons over tomorrow morning," Lizabeth promised. "And I'll fix your hair a special way. I'll bring my curling iron, too."

Rose passed over two green berries, the only ones left on a branch. "I think the birds came before we did."

"No, look, there are some good bushes back here," Kat called.

The other girls scrambled through the underbrush to join her. They picked silently for a while.

"I know!" Hannah suddenly exclaimed. "I want red-white-and-blue *hair*!"

"Don't be so silly," Amanda said.

"Why *can't* I have red-white-and-blue hair? Why can't I?"

Lizabeth laughed. "That *would* be different. I mean, if someone wants to stand out. . . ."

"Hannah is determined to be the star of the show," Kat said. "And why not?"

"That's crazy! I'm *not* going to dye my little sister's hair," Amanda said. "Hannah, you're not going through the rest of the summer with red-white-and-blue hair!"

"What if it's something that washes out right away?" Kat suggested. "Her hair is so light, color would show up on it very easily. It would be fun for the Fourth of July and then she'd wash it out that night."

"I don't know," Amanda frowned. "What would I use?"

"Paint?" Lizabeth asked.

"My watercolors wouldn't show up well," Kat said. "Unless we used up a whole tube for each color and that's way too expensive. It should be something thicker, like oil paint."

"Would oil paint wash out right away?" Amanda asked.

"I don't think so," Kat admitted. "Anyway, I don't have any."

"Forget it. I'm not taking a chance with my sister's hair," Amanda said.

"Let me think." Rose looked at Hannah sympathetically. "It would be fun to have something more than a white sheet."

Hannah pouted. "I want red-white-and-blue hair."

"I know!" Lizabeth exclaimed. "Look at her mouth!"

Hannah guiltily covered her mouthful of berries, but not before the girls saw the blue juice all around it.

"*Blue*berries!" Lizabeth said. "And there are raspberries growing wild near the Mill Pond. *Red* raspberries!"

"Fruit juice is harmless," Rose said. "It's nothing like paint or dye."

"And for the white, we can mix a paste from flour," Lizabeth said. "How simple is that?"

"It would make it more of a costume . . ." Amanda said.

Hannah clapped her hands. "Yes, yes, yes!"

On the morning of July Fourth, Kat came to Amanda's kitchen with a basket of blueberries. Lizabeth brought the wild raspberries. Rose carried a mortar and pestle.

"What's that?" Amanda asked.

"My father uses it to crush pills into a powder when he's giving medication to his patients," Rose explained. "I thought it would be good for crushing the berries."

"Perfect!" Lizabeth said.

They worked on the flour first. Hannah stepped on Kat's foot and then Amanda's, in her eagerness to get close to the counter and see everything. They mixed the flour in a bowl with water until it turned into a thick white paste.

"Well, that worked," Kat said with satisfaction.

"That's the easy part," Amanda said. *Everyone* knew how to make a paste of flour and water!

Rose crushed batches of blueberries in the mortar with the pestle and poured them into another bowl. "Hmmm, too liquid."

"We'll add some flour paste," Lizabeth said. She stirred in a little of it and examined the result. The blueberries had thickened nicely. "Not too lumpy. And the color is even better."

"That's a pretty color blue," Hannah agreed.

"Now for the raspberries," Rose said.

The raspberries needed thickening too and they added just a little flour paste to their bowl, one teaspoon at a time, so that the mixture wouldn't lighten too much.

"We'd better stop," Kat said. "That's a nice light-red right now. We really don't want *pink*."

Lizabeth frowned. "It's more liquid than the blueberries."

Amanda stirred the mixture. "It's not quite as thick,

but it shouldn't run. Good enough to coat her hair."

"For once—success!" Kat exclaimed.

"Success!" Hannah echoed.

The girls smiled at each other. They remembered their last disastrous concoction—the horrible chocolate ice cream drink that they'd made the year before—and this success was sweet.

"We have plenty of time before the pageant," Amanda said.

"Are you going to color my hair now?" Hannah was excited.

"Put on your white sheet first," Rose said. "So getting it over your head won't be a problem."

"And bring your brush down," Lizabeth added.

Hannah ran up the stairs and clattered down with the sheet floating from her shoulders. She held up her hairbrush.

Amanda made some adjustments and then tied the costume into place with a wide sash she had made from more sheeting. "All right, now you're a white stripe."

"Let's put towels around her, in case of drips," Rose said.

"We have to part her hair into three separate sections," Lizabeth said. "Do you have some rubber bands?"

Amanda reached into a kitchen drawer. "Here."

"Ouch," Hannah protested as Lizabeth fastened the sections tightly.

"What color should we do first?" Kat asked.

"It doesn't matter. We'll have to keep them separate, that's all." Lizabeth was automatically put in charge; she was the expert at arranging hair.

Amanda took a nervous breath. "Now?"

Lizabeth nodded. "Now."

Amanda dipped the hairbrush in the blueberry mix. Slowly, carefully, she brushed it onto the left side section. Some more, then a little more. . . ."Whew, that came out really blue!"

"White next." Kat rinsed the brush in the sink and dried it. Then she applied the flour mixture neatly as the middle stripe, just a hairbreadth from the blue.

"Great," Rose said. "Kat has a steady hand."

"Because she's an artist," Amanda said. "Do the red, too, Kat."

Kat applied the raspberry mixture, again leaving a very narrow separation between the colors. "What do you think? Do I need more?"

"No, it's good," Lizabeth said. "Let's quit while we're ahead."

"I want to see! I want to see!" Hannah started to jump but Lizabeth firmly held down her shoulder.

"Don't move! You have to let it dry," Lizabeth told her.

"Don't *move*?" Hannah asked in a small voice.

"It's worth it, pumpkin," Amanda said. "Your hair is definitely red, white, and blue!"

Hannah obediently stood very still. It was hard for her. "Is it all right if I breathe?"

Amanda laughed. "Yes, I think you'd better breathe."

"But don't move your head at all," Lizabeth warned.

Hannah took shallow breaths. Her arms were tight at her sides. She held her head stiffly. "My neck is hurting," she whimpered.

"You should be dry soon," Rose comforted her.

After a while, Lizabeth tested the raspberry-red section with the tip of her finger. "Ready." She removed the rubber bands cautiously.

Hannah's hair was divided into thick, pasty colored stripes. The few little lumps were barely noticeable.

"Excellent!" Kat exclaimed.

"Very patriotic!" Lizabeth said.

"I want to see." Hannah started to head upstairs.

"Wait, I have a mirror here." Lizabeth took a silver compact out of her purse, snapped it open and handed it to Hannah.

Hannah stared into the little mirror, transfixed. She broke into a big smile. "It's good. It's better than Betsy Ross's cap!"

Amanda, Hannah, Kat, Rose, and Lizabeth walked along Lighthouse Lane toward the village green. They passed the elderly Peabody sisters on their way and then the Crimmins family. Everyone smiled at Hannah.

"Now there's a nice little patriot," Mr. Crimmins said.

Hannah beamed.

They turned onto East Street. They could see the blankets and lawn chairs that dotted the square of lawn, ready for the children's pageant and the annual band concert that would follow.

Hannah walked proudly, with her head high. Amanda was pleased. It was so nice when everything worked out as planned!

The trouble didn't start until they passed the rose-bushes at the side of Lizabeth's house. First there was loud buzzing and then Hannah crying "Amanda!"

Bees were leaving the roses to surround Hannah's hair.

"Don't do anything! Stand still!" Amanda was protectively at her sister's side, but what could she do? If she swatted them, the bees would be *angry*!

A bee alighted on Hannah's red stripe.

"I'm scared," Hannah moaned.

"Don't do anything. They won't hurt you if you don't bother them." Amanda's shaky voice didn't go with her words.

"The berries are attracting them," Kat said. "Let's walk away *slowly*. Very *calmly*."

The girls walked at an unnaturally slow pace. The bees followed easily. They buzzed mostly around Hannah's head. She looked terrified and gripped Amanda's hand. One or two bees investigated the other girls.

"I'm *allergic*," Rose said. "I was stung once and my arm swelled up *triple*! I—I *have* to get away."

"Just walk away from Hannah," Kat advised.

Rose had spotted the hose set up to sprinkle the Merchants' front lawn. "They—they don't go in water. Do they?" She dashed onto the grass and into the spray.

Hannah, panicked, ran into the spray, too.

"No, Hannah!" Lizabeth screamed.

"Come back, Hannah!" Amanda called.

It was too late. Hannah's hair had been watered.

The bees were gone. Rose and Hannah returned to stand on the pavement of Lighthouse Lane. The other girls stared at Hannah in horror.

The red, white, and blue stripes had flowed together. Hannah's hair was a lumpy mass of purple, shading from violet to a deeper hue. Rivulets of color ran along her forehead and down the top of the white sheet.

"What happened?" Hannah looked from one face to another. "What's the matter?"

Kat, Amanda, Rose, and Lizabeth couldn't answer. They looked at each other, full of apprehension and guilt. What had they done? How would poor Hannah take this?

"Let me see," Hannah said.

Lizabeth slowly, very slowly, withdrew her compact and handed it over.

The girls stopped breathing as Hannah clicked it open. They braced themselves for a terrible, heartbreaking wail.

Hannah stared into the mirror. Her eyes widened in surprise. Her mouth opened into a huge silent O.

Their eyes focused on Hannah. Amanda's stomach clenched.

Hannah's shoulders began to shake. Amanda extended her hand but—Hannah was *laughing*!

"Oh, my!" Hannah's shoulders shook with *giggles*! "My hair turned purple."

That freed the other girls to break into roars of relieved laughter. "Very purple," Kat gasped.

"It looks so *funny*!" Hannah laughed.

When they finally quieted down, Kat, Lizabeth, Rose, and Amanda contributed their clean handkerchiefs to wiping Hannah's face. There was nothing they could do about her hair.

"Who'd expect a six-year-old to have a sense of humor," Kat said. "You're terrific, Hannah-banana!"

Amanda smiled in agreement.

"My favorite little girl," Rose added.

"You'll definitely stand out," Lizabeth whispered in Hannah's ear.

The children's pageant was as cute as ever. When Hannah marched on, she was a purple dot in the white stripes. But it was no worse than Mary Margaret turning left instead of right and marching in the wrong direction. Or Betsy Ross forgetting to give the flag to George Washington until he stamped his foot and grabbed it from her. Amanda could hear Hannah over the other children, singing "Yankee Doodle" loud and true. Father had come just in time and he applauded enthusiastically with everyone else.

He turned to Amanda. "Is there any special reason why your sister's hair is purple?"

"No special reason," Amanda murmured. "Just the sum of red, white, and blue."

Later they listened to the annual band concert. Hannah, worn out and happy, curled up on their blanket next to Father.

In the evening, everyone in town headed for the docks. A barge on the water set off fireworks. There were a multitude of "ooohs" and "aaahs" all around as red and blue sparklers burst overhead. The fireworks were breathtaking, but no more so than the brilliant stars in the velvet summer sky and the full moon reflected in the waves. Thank you, God, Amanda thought. I'm proud to be an American and happy to live in Cape Light.

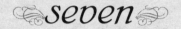

Thursday evening, Amanda looked across the dinner table at Father. In the mellow glow of the Forbeses' dining room, the lines in his face had disappeared. He looked especially relaxed.

Mrs. Forbes had placed Reverend Morgan next to Mrs. Cornell. What was she doing here, anyway? Rose had said it would be just family. Mrs. Cornell might be Mrs. Forbes's best friend, but that didn't make her *family*! All through the fish course, Mrs. Cornell had chattered about English antiques, and Father had seemed entranced, though as far as Amanda knew, he didn't have the least interest in old furniture! Of course, he was a master at listening, with total attention, to the most boring of parishoners.

"That looks delicious!" Mrs. Cornell said as Edna carried the platter of roast beef around the table.

"Edna is a gem," Mrs. Forbes said, and the cook

blushed with pleasure. "We're so lucky to have her."

Father, serving himself, looked across at Amanda and winked. She smiled back. On their way across the street to the Forbes home, they had both wished out loud for roast duck with orange sauce again. Of course, the roast beef was a treat, too, especially since it was accompanied by the savory gravy that Amanda had no idea how to make.

Amanda didn't like to cook. It was messy and tiring and there was always burnt-on food in the pots and a lengthy clean-up. Sometimes she thought she might try something from her mother's old recipe box, but she'd wind up serving Hannah and Father the quickest and simplest of meals. No wonder Father enjoyed dinner invitations from the Forbeses so much. Maybe tomorrow she'd really look through the recipes. . . .

"Cut the meat for me, Amanda?" Hannah asked. All traces of purple had washed out of her hair last night and she looked sweet with shining braids.

Amanda got up and went around the table to her sister. Hannah was sitting on Father's other side and he hadn't made a move to help her. He was too busy chatting with Mrs. Cornell! But Hannah did ask for me, Amanda thought as she cut the beef into neat bite-sized pieces, and anyway, Father doesn't know how she wants it. Amanda was careful to keep the pieces of meat separate from the mashed potatoes. Hannah didn't like one kind of food touching another on her plate. Men don't understand the silly food quirks that young children have, Amanda thought.

Silver scraped against china as everyone ate contentedly.

"We saw the strangest thing at the lighthouse a few days ago. Whales blowing!" Rose said. She was always at ease at dinner conversations, Amanda thought. Her parents didn't believe that children should be seen but not heard, or mustn't speak until they were spoken to, as so many others did.

"That's interesting. Are you sure?" Mrs. Cornell asked.

"We saw the water spout through binoculars," Rose explained, "and Kat was sure it was whales."

"I thought they'd been hunted almost to extinction along this coast," Mrs. Cornell said. "It would be nice if they were coming back. But so close to shore? That *is* odd."

"You sound as though you know a bit about them," Dr. Forbes said. "Coming from New York, Miranda and I are familiar with the wildlife in Central Park and that's about all."

"Is there wildlife in Central Park?" Amanda was surprised.

Rose laughed. "Pigeons, sparrows, and some very aggressive squirrels. Though there are always rumors about exotic species hidden away. Like in the New York sewers."

"I've been reading about whales for a while," Mrs. Cornell said. "They're gentle giants, not at all the menacing beasts they've been painted. They stick together in big groups—I guess you'd call them sociable—and they seem to have real feelings for each other."

"That's fascinating, Doris." Father said. "It's hard to imagine underwater creatures with feelings."

Doris! And was Father truly *fascinated* by this? Amanda wondered. It seemed to her that Mrs. Cornell was lecturing them like a schoolteacher.

"They're not actually *fish*," Mrs. Cornell said. "They're mammals, like us. Pilot whales carry their babies for up to sixteen months, they nurse their young, and then the calves often stay alongside their mothers long after weaning."

Amanda was only half-listening. She wanted to add

something about whales—not that she knew a thing about them—just so she could start with "Jed Langford said" or "Jed Langford told me." How badly she wanted to say his name aloud!

"That makes whales sound—" Mrs. Forbes interrupted herself with a laugh. "I was going to say 'almost human'!"

"Apparently they have a very high level of intelligence," Mrs. Cornell went on. "Some naturalists believe that they communicate with each other underwater. With whale songs." She smiled. "Now that sounds a bit too imaginative, even to me. Naturalists disagree all the time and it's hard to know which books to take seriously."

Father smiled at her. "Well, I knew you had an interest in history . . . and now a student of nature, too? I'm impressed."

"Don't be." Mrs. Cornell smiled back. She had deep dimples. "I'm surrounded by books, don't forget, and when business is slow—as unfortunately it often is—I read. And read and read."

"Then I'd definitely call you well-read," Father said. His eyes were twinkling.

Was Father really taken with Mrs. Cornell? Amanda wondered. She had a pleasant appearance, though she certainly wasn't a great beauty like Rose's mother. Mrs. Cornell wasn't young, her face was too round, and there was a small gap between her front teeth. On the plus side, she did have an engaging smile, a peaches-and-cream complexion, and large, long-lashed brown eyes that were emphasized by the brown plaid shirtwaist she was wearing.

After dessert the gentlemen did not retreat to the parlor for cigars and brandy, as they would anywhere else. By now, Amanda and her father were used to Mrs. Forbes's unconventional ways as a hostess. She kept everyone together at the dining table and served brandy right there to Dr. Forbes. Reverend Morgan, of course, did not drink or smoke, but Dr. Forbes lit a pipe.

The conversation veered toward President Teddy Roosevelt and politics. Amanda stifled a yawn. Rose helped Edna bring plates back to the kitchen and Amanda got up and carried the bowl with the remains of the dessert.

Rose yanked Amanda into the pantry. "I think it's working," she whispered.

"What?" Amanda asked.

"My mother's matchmaking."

So that's what was going on! That's why Mrs. Cornell

had been invited with them. *"Matchmaking?"* It sounded all wrong, almost common, in connection with Father.

"Well, not exactly," Rose laughed, "but they seemed to get along so well the last time you were here, and then Mrs. Cornell said your father stopped in at the bookstore more often than usual, so Mother thought she'd give them another opportunity. . . . My mother's such a romantic!"

"She is," Amanda agreed. Father was being polite, she thought; he would never embarrass Mrs. Cornell. But in spite of Mrs. Forbes's romantic fantasies, Father didn't have any spare time and he was still grieving, just as she was. Her mother was not and could not be forgotten, Amanda told herself.

At the end of the evening, after all the thank-yous and good-byes had been said, Mrs. Cornell walked outside with Amanda, Hannah, and Father.

"Your carriage isn't in front," Father said.

"No. It was so beautiful tonight, I decided to walk," Mrs. Cornell said.

"Then I'll see you home," Father offered.

"It's really not necessary. . . ."

"Oh, but it is! I need to walk off that roast beef and Yorkshire pudding!" Father smiled. "If you don't mind taking my two ladies home first."

They all crossed the street to Amanda's house and Father opened the front door with a flourish. "Good night, girls."

"Good night," Mrs. Cornell said. She leaned forward and gave both Hannah and Amanda an impulsive kiss on the cheek. Surprised, Amanda withdrew, but Hannah seemed to curl toward Mrs. Cornell. "Reverend Morgan is lucky to have such lovely daughters!"

"Thank you," Amanda mumbled.

Hannah was already in bed and fast asleep by the time Amanda heard Father open the door. It would have been nice if he had been home in time to kiss Hannah good night, Amanda thought. Hannah had waited up as long as she could keep her eyes open. The walk to Mrs. Cornell's apartment over the Pelican Book Shop couldn't take more than ten minutes, Amanda thought, but almost two hours had gone by.

Amanda met Father in the kitchen. "Hannah wanted to say good night to you."

"Oh, yes, of course. Next time. I meant to come back immediately, but Mrs. Cornell invited me in for chamomile tea and I noticed her collection of Audubon prints and we got to talking. . . ."

It was nice to see Father look happy, Amanda

thought. She would never begrudge him that.

"Then I guess you don't want any more tea." Amanda sat down opposite him at the table.

"No, thank you. . . . Doris is a remarkable woman."

"Is she?"

"Most women in her position, widowed without means, would have gone to live with relatives as an unpaid governess or tutor or housekeeper. And Doris's house was mostly owned by the bank, so she was in a terrible situation. But she converted the downstairs of the house into the bookstore and has made a success of it. She's quite the enterprising businesswoman."

"You always say a woman's highest calling is to be a wife and mother," Amanda reminded him.

"Yes, but I admire Doris's courage and initiative in the face of disaster."

"And you don't even seem to mind Mrs. Forbes's suffragette opinions. Tonight at dinner—"

"I have no objection to women getting the vote, if it doesn't interfere with their roles as wives and mothers. Though Mrs. Forbes is a little too strident about it for my taste."

"She gets away with it because she's so beautiful," Amanda said.

"Doris holds some of the same opinions, but she's soft-spoken, with that natural sweetness of hers." Father smiled. "It goes down better with sugar than Mrs. Forbes's vinegar."

"I never knew Mrs. Cornell's name was Doris," Amanda said.

"Yes, Doris." Father smiled and his eyes were full of light. "So it was an altogether nice evening, don't you think? Though our prayers for duck with orange sauce weren't answered this time."

Amanda smiled back, but she felt uneasy. She loved Father with all her heart and it was nice to see him looking openly happy. Any other man left with a seven-year-old and a newborn would have sent them away to be raised by relatives. He had to feel terribly burdened, but he did his duty.

Amanda had a vague memory of long, warm evenings at home, with Mama and Father playing cards with her at the rickety little table.

If Mrs. Cornell—Doris—could bring his lonely days to an end, well, that was a good thing, wasn't it? But he hardly gave any time to her and Hannah as it was. If Mrs. Cornell took even more of his time, they'd be on the verge of losing their one remaining parent.

Mrs. Cornell came to lunch after church on July eighth. She carried a huge basket of fried chicken and biscuits, as if Amanda wasn't capable of providing a meal for Father and Hannah!

Later in the week, Mrs. Cornell brought curtains of white cotton woven with red roosters that she had sewn to replace the ancient ones covering their kitchen window. It was true that the old ones, once moss-green, had faded to a dull grayish hue, but Amanda's *mother* had made them. They had been hemmed by her own mother's hands!

Father helped Mrs. Cornell attach them to the window. Amanda would never have imagined Father fumbling with window rods and laughing!

Mrs. Cornell stepped back. "There! That's cheerful, isn't it?"

Amanda simmered while Father and Hannah applauded how nice the new curtains looked.

Of course Amanda wanted Father to be happy, but she had had quite enough of Mrs. Cornell!

eight

July 10, 1906

Dear Jed,

It's so cruel to be kept apart this way. My friend Joanna Mason from school is having a hayride the night of July thirteenth. Her father is a farmer, so she has the big wagon and the hay. All the upper graders in our class are invited. Rose asked Joanna if she could invite Chris Merchant, and Joanna said yes. Rose and Chris Merchant—that's Lizabeth's older brother—have been keeping company for a while. I didn't like him much, he seemed to me a spoiled rich man's son, but I think Rose changed him for the better. They're courting openly, for all the world to see, and I try not to be envious. It's true that Rose is already fourteen, but still . . . It's easier for her because Mrs. Forbes has all sorts of modern ways.

I wish I could ask you to come to the hayride with me. I keep thinking of Romeo and Juliet. *We studied it in school last term. She wasn't supposed to be with him because of his name! That seems even more unreasonable than being kept apart because of my age, doesn't it? Father is a great admirer of William Shakespeare. He has volumes of his work on the shelves in the study and quotes from him in his sermons sometimes. So I mentioned to Father that though they're famous lovers, Juliet was very young. Thirteen, I think, like me. Father wouldn't answer me. He refused to talk to me about it and it made me so angry. I have to pray to keep anger out of my heart.*

Love, Amanda

July 13, 1906
My beautiful Amanda,

I guess you're going on the hayride tonight and without me. I wish I could see you under the stars, outshining every one of them.

I don't know that book Romeo and Juliet, *but it sounds like they're in the same pickle as us.*

*Here's what I'm thinking: Being separated for a
long whaling voyage, on top of having to wait
until you're fifteen or sixteen—that's too long
and too hard. Did you know that captains and
first mates of whalers often bring their wives
and even children along? I don't think everyone
in the crew is allowed to, but if I work real hard,
and I will, I'll make first mate. What I want to
know is—would you do that? Would you want to
be the first mate's wife and live on a whaler?
Then we'd be together with both of us having a
great adventure. Write me your answer so I can
dream about it.*

Love, Jed

Yes, yes, yes! She'd write her answer when she
came home tonight, when she had loads of time to luxu-
riate in every word!

She had to get Hannah ready for the hayride now.
She riffled through Hannah's closet. She pulled out a
navy wool jacket and a knit scarf.

"I don't want to wear a jacket!" Hannah protested.

"It's sure to turn chilly in the evening," Amanda
said.

91

"But it's too hot *now*!"

"Then don't wear it, just carry it. So you'll have it if—"

"I don't *want* to carry anything!"

Amanda sighed. "All right, I'll hold it for you." Hannah was being difficult because she was nervous and excited about going with the older group, Amanda thought. "Come on, Hannah-banana, change into your wool skirt, all right? They'll be coming soon."

Hannah would be the only little child there and, though Amanda didn't like to admit it, it was burdensome to bring her along. Father had the church council meeting tonight, but it wasn't fair that he just assumed she'd take care of Hannah. It was true there wasn't anyone else, but other arrangements could have been made if he'd tried. . . .

Amanda went to her own room. She was dressed and ready, she had braided Hannah's hair, and all she had to do was wait for her sister to finish dressing. She had time to read Jed's note once more.

She took the packet of letters from the bottom of her glove drawer and settled down on her bed. She untied the blue ribbon and unfolded the page she had retrieved that afternoon. "Would you want to be the first mate's wife and live on a whaler?" ". . . we'd be together with both of us having a great adventure."

Her heart jumped at the thought of it. She wasn't going to be the only one of her friends to remain ordinary after all. Yes, she'd choose adventure—and Jed! Amanda Morgan, sailing around the world. Amanda Langford!

Her three best friends had such strong directions. Kat had the talent for art and the determination to make her name as a painter. Rose, always horse-crazy, now shared a dream with Chris Merchant—to have a ranch out west someday, where they'd train and breed horses.

And Lizabeth was no longer shallow and snobbish, without a thought in her curly blond head beyond the latest fashion. On that long night when Lizabeth went missing while Tracy was so sick, something had turned her around. She was serious about going to medical school someday—a truly astounding ambition for a girl! She was reading every science book that Dr. Forbes recommended, full of words that Amanda couldn't understand at all.

I'll never be as smart as Lizabeth, Amanda thought, or as talented as Kat or as brave as Rose. But Jed has saved me from being dull and ordinary.

Amanda couldn't resist reading that last note once again. Just touching the notepaper made her fingertips tingle! "My beautiful Amanda, I guess you're going on the hayride tonight . . ."

The hayride! It seemed like everything happened at once. The squeal of the hay wagon's wheels stopping in front of her house. "Amanda! Come on, Amanda!" And Hannah's plaintive cry, "My shoelace broke!"

"Oh, Hannah!" Amanda rushed into her room. "They're all waiting for us out front!"

Amanda hastily undid Hannah's ankle-high lace-up shoe. She double-knotted the tie where it had broken and relaced it. She grabbed Hannah's jacket and scarf. "Come on, let's go!" They ran down the stairs and to the wagon where Amanda's laughing classmates boosted them aboard.

Joanna's father held the reins and the dappled mare slowly pulled the wagon along Lighthouse Lane under a twilight sky.

Everyone was excited and talking all at once. Some of the seventh and eighth graders hadn't seen each other since school ended. And here they were, out together after dark! There was a lot of wriggling, and throwing popcorn. And over and above all else, Grace's screeching giggle as Arthur stuffed hay down the back of her dress.

Mark, John, and Vernon were acting stupid. They were trying to bury Kat and Lizabeth under the hay.

None of the boys were teasing her, Amanda thought, because they respected that she was taking care of Hannah. Not that she'd want them to, they were all too silly. But somehow it made her feel *old*.

"Cut it out—you're making me sneeze," Lizabeth protested, laughing.

Kat threw a handful of hay at Mark and it stuck comically to his dark hair. Of course, that made him twist her arm until she said "uncle."

Hannah leaned against Amanda's knees. "Is Kat fighting with Mark?" she whispered.

"No, they're just playing," Amanda said.

Hannah's being good, Amanda thought, though she's completely out of place. It's not Hannah's fault. She'll get sleepy long before we come home, but she's really very good.

"Look everybody, there's the Big Dipper," Kat said.

Amanda tilted her head up. It had turned dark and the constellations were dazzlingly clear. There was Orion . . . and an almost full moon. . . .

Amanda shifted on the pile of sweet-smelling hay.

Some of the stalks were sticking into her skirt. She swayed gently with the rocking of the wagon.

Rose sat with Chris Merchant. His arm was around her shoulders. He whispered something into her ear and Rose nodded. Amanda had to look away. She wanted Jed's arm around her. Kat and Lizabeth don't mind being without a special boy tonight, Amanda thought, because they haven't found one yet. But I have.

Everyone quieted down and settled into comfortable spots as the evening went on.

Johnny Alveira's pairing up with Mabel, Amanda thought, if letting her wear his red-and-black checked jacket means anything. Or maybe she's cold and he's being a gentleman.

The horse trotted steadily along. They sang rounds of "Row Your Boat" that finally sputtered into silence. Popcorn and peanuts were passed around. Hannah's head was heavy on Amanda's knees.

"Are you falling asleep, Hannah-banana?"

"No," Hannah mumbled, with half-closed eyes.

Joanna began "Shine On Harvest Moon," hopelessly off-key but enthusiastic. Everyone joined in, clapping in time to the part about having no loving since "January, February, June and July . . ." Amanda took over the melody and the others followed her. "Snow time ain't no time to sit outdoors and spoon . . ." Lizabeth tried to harmonize. Amanda stopped singing by the second chorus. Loving, spoon, moon . . . People had to be spooning everywhere if it turned up in all the song lyrics. Maybe even Father and Mrs. Cornell, though that was almost impossible to imagine! Why was love allowed for everyone else in the world and forbidden to her? Amanda sat still and sad in the midst of her clapping, singing classmates.

The wagon stopped off in front of Amanda's house.

Father had left the hall and parlor lights on for them, Amanda noticed. Hannah was stiff-legged with sleepiness and Amanda helped her down. Rose took one last, lingering look at Chris and she jumped down, too.

"That was fun." Rose stretched. "I'm *covered* with hay, but I'm too tired for a bath tonight."

"I know," Amanda said. "I think I'll skip Hannah's, too."

Rose gave her a searching look. "Amanda—I'm sorry. It's not easy for you, is it?"

"It's all right." Amanda said. "No, really. I got the most wonderful letter this afternoon! You can't imagine. . . ."

Hannah sagged against her and she sighed. "We have to go in. I'll tell you about it later."

"Good night. See you tomorrow." Rose ran across the street.

"Good night."

Amanda stepped inside and blinked in the harsh light of the hall. She had one hand in Hannah's and was about to put out the gaslight with the other when she heard the creak of the parlor sofa. Father strode into the hall.

"Father!" She was surprised. He hardly ever sat in the parlor and it was rather late.

"Hannah, go upstairs. Immediately please," he said.

"Amanda has to put me to bed," Hannah whined.

"Go on," Father ordered. "She'll come up later."

They watched Hannah dragging herself up the stairs. She pulled herself along by the banister and her shoes scraped against each step. It would be nice if Father kissed her good night, Amanda thought. She glanced at him. He looked stern and unbending.

"Hannah was very well behaved, though it went past her bedtime," Amanda said. "It was a beautiful night. We saw the constellations clear as anything and—"

"Come into the parlor," Father interrupted her. He

led the way and Amanda followed, puzzled. Logs crackled in the fireplace. They hardly ever set a fire in the parlor. Was the chimney clear? Amanda worried. When did I last call a chimney sweep?

"What do you have to say for yourself?" Father's voice was harsh. Something was definitely wrong.

And then, on the sofa, heaped in a pile, she saw Jed's letters! Her blue ribbons snaked across the maroon velvet cushions. Amanda's hand automatically went to her heart as her blood froze.

nine

"My letters!" Amanda gasped.

"The Langford boy's letters." Father's mouth twisted with distaste as he said Jed's name. "And quite a large volume. I assume that means you've been writing to him, too."

Amanda bit her lip and nodded.

"In direct defiance of my wishes," Father continued.

"You said I couldn't see him and I haven't. You never said I couldn't *write*," Amanda said.

"When I told you no contact, did I really need to add no letters or no telegrams or no smoke signals or—"

"No, sir." Amanda looked down at the floor. Father's sarcasm was painful. But then she raised her head and met his steely eyes. "They were in my *drawer*! They were at the bottom of my glove drawer! How could you—"

"You should know me better than that," Father

interrupted her. "They were scattered all over your bed, and when I went in to turn off the light—you ran out and left the light on—I couldn't very well miss them."

"Oh." With Hannah's shoelace problem and everyone calling her, she had run downstairs for the hayride and forgotten to put the letters away! And in the last one, she recalled, Jed had asked if she would want to live with him on a whaler. She was going to write her answer tonight. She'd been planning to start with, "Dear Jed, Yes, yes, yes!"

Father was studying her face. Amanda tried to keep her expression blank.

"I didn't read them," Father said. "I would never stoop that low. But I couldn't help seeing his signature. 'All my love, Jed.' All my love indeed! Exactly what has been going on here?"

"Nothing. Nothing at all but letters."

"I'd like to be able to believe that," Father said.

"It's the truth." Father was almost calling her a liar! Amanda swallowed. "Though he does love me."

"Nonsense. You're such an innocent. A boy will say and do just about anything if he wants to keep company with a girl."

"I do believe he loves me," Amanda repeated stubbornly. "And I love him. What's so wrong about that?"

"You're much too young to know what love is," Father said. "You have no idea. And you betrayed my trust. If you can't see what's wrong with that. . . ." Father shook his head. "I expected far more of you."

"Maybe you expect too much of me," Amanda whispered.

"Really? Good character and honesty—is that expecting too much?"

"No," Amanda mumbled.

"And for this!" Father waved a letter in his hand. "Shabby notepaper. What kind of respect for you does that show?"

"He doesn't have the money for fancy stationery!"

"Penmanship like chicken scratches."

"I don't care what his handwriting looks like! It's what he writes that counts!"

"Amanda, please stop shouting. I'd be embarrassed to have Hannah learn about your behavior."

The last bit of spirit left Amanda. He made her feel small and ashamed.

"Come over here, Amanda."

Amanda took a step toward Father. He had never hit her, never once for any reason, but as she came close to him, she couldn't help flinching.

He handed her a bunch of letters and nodded toward the fireplace. "Destroy them."

"Oh, no, please, no. . . ."

"I want them out of this house and out of your mind."

"No, please don't make me. . . ."

"Amanda!"

"Please, Father!"

"Go on!"

Her precious letters! Under Father's stern eye, she dropped the first letter into the fire and watched it turn brown and crumple into ash. Another and then another burned in front of her eyes. It became too painful to destroy them one by one. She threw them into the fire in bunches, to be finished with it. The forget-me-not blue ribbon curled into the flame. When there was nothing left, she stared into the heap of ashes. I'll remember, she thought, I'll remember every beautiful word.

"Very well, that's done," Father said. "Let that be the end of it."

He turned away and headed down the hall. She heard his footsteps, heavy on the stairs. Amanda felt as if she had been whipped.

Amanda had to tell Jed. She couldn't bear the thought of him looking day after day for a note in the cave and never finding one.

She wouldn't, she *couldn't* write to him again. She had wrestled with it all day Saturday. Father was the spiritual guide for almost everyone in Cape Light. If he saw character defects in her, maybe he was right. Somehow she had to win back his good opinion. Somehow she had to make Jed understand. No more letters, but at the same time she would give him her answer: Yes, she wanted to live on a whaler with him someday! If he cared enough for her to wait. . . .

Sunday morning at church was her only opportunity to talk to Jed, at least for a moment. Father had left for church early. When Amanda entered with Hannah, Father was near the altar, chatting with Mr. Alveira and the choirmaster.

She saw Jed sitting in a row near the back. His face lit up as their eyes connected.

"Go on ahead." Amanda gave Hannah a small nudge down the aisle. "Sit down. I'll be right there."

She watched Hannah heading for their usual place near the front. She stopped in the aisle at Jed's row. "Jed?"

He sprang to his feet. "Excuse me. Excuse me, ma'am." He seemed to be one huge smile as he made his way to her, past the knees of other parishioners.

"Morning, Amanda!" The happy lilt in his voice broke her heart.

"My father found out," Amanda said. "We can't write anymore."

Jed's face dropped. "You mean about the cave? Don't worry, I'll think of someplace else."

Father was looking directly at her now and frowning. She had to be quick!

"No. No more letters. I'm not allowed." To be so very close to Jed and have nothing good to say! Oh, but she did, she'd give him her answer now. Amanda started to tell him. "But I do want to—"

Jed interrupted. "No meetings, and no *letters*! That leaves nothing! What's wrong with letters, anyway?" His eyes had narrowed and turned cold. "Does he think I'll *contaminate* you with the paper? Does it smell too *fishy* to him?"

"No Jed, it's—"

"Well, I'll tell you something. My family doesn't approve of you, either." He was almost shouting and the people nearby stared. He noticed and lowered his voice, but his tone remained icy. "'Too rich for your blood,' they tell me. 'Not fit for a fisherman's son.'"

"We're not rich." Amanda was stung. "Our house belongs to the church and—"

He was too angry to listen. "They've seen you around town with that banker's daughter in her fancy silks and satins. . . ."

"Lizabeth? She's not like—"

"I don't care about that. And I hardly care if your father thinks I'm not good enough. I only need to know one thing." He looked so deeply into Amanda's eyes that she felt seared. "Tell me right now. Are you going to obey him?"

Amanda lowered her head. "Yes. I have to. But—"

"All right, fine, obey him!" Jed exploded. "I've had enough. I'm tired of accepting crumbs!"

He swept past her and stormed up the aisle and out of the church.

She stood still, distressed, too shocked to move. People were looking at her. Father watched her from the front of the chapel, his eyebrows raised.

Amanda pulled herself together. She walked down the aisle toward the empty space next to her little sister. Hannah was leaning against Mrs. Cornell on her other side. Amanda took a deep breath and sank into her seat. Mrs. Cornell must have noticed the disturbance. She reached across Hannah and sympathetically squeezed Amanda's hand. Amanda jerked her hand away.

I wanted to say that I'd go on a whaler with him, anytime, anywhere. . . . And if it took a long time for him to become first mate or captain, I'd wait until he could take me along. I was planning to say that I'd wait for him forever and a day.

What now? Amanda felt entirely lost.

ten

"He told me he had a quick temper," Amanda confided to Rose, "but I never thought he would turn it on me."

"Don't look so sad." Rose's dark eyes were full of empathy. "I'll bet anything he comes to church next Sunday and says he's sorry."

Jed didn't show up at church the next Sunday.

Summer came late to Massachusetts, but it became blistering hot very quickly. Amanda went to the swimming hole in the woods with Hannah, Kat, and Kat's younger brothers, Todd and Jamie.

"Don't tell Ma," Kat warned before she climbed up to the high rocks from which only the oldest boys dared dive.

Amanda held her breath as Kat came hurtling down into the water. It was scary. The skirt of Kat's bathing costume tangled around her legs. Amanda was used to Kat's daredevil ways, but she couldn't help worrying. "You could have tripped!"

Kat laughed, climbed the rocks, and jumped down again. Todd worried, too. "I'll tell Ma if you don't stop!" he yelled. Amanda was relieved when Kat finally settled down.

Amanda slipped out of the heat and into the water, but she couldn't stay in. The hole's dark depths were icy. She lay back on a low, flat rock, maneuvering into just the right position to let her feet dip in and stay wet.

On another afternoon when Cape Light shimmered in the heat, Amanda, Kat, Rose, and Lizabeth gathered in the lighthouse tower. With the huge windows all around open to any possible breeze, it was the coolest place in town. They hadn't played jacks for a long time, but suddenly it became a passion again. They played until the longer day's light faded and Kat had to start her evening watch.

Amanda couldn't resist checking the cave on her way home in the twilight. Just in case . . . There was nothing.

On a long, lazy summer evening, Amanda sipped lemonade with Lizabeth on the Merchants' front porch. They helped Hannah catch fireflies in a jar, but Amanda made her free them before they died. They watched townspeople going by on their after-dinner walks around the village green. Father and Mrs. Cornell strolled by, grinning at each other. Amanda didn't know where to look.

Jed didn't show up on the following Sunday or the one after that. Father gave a fine sermon. Amanda sang with the choir. And all she could think of was the empty space Jed had left behind.

Dear God, Amanda prayed, please help me to stop missing him. She thought she'd always remember this summer as the one marked by the absence of letters.

The girls gathered in the lighthouse tower after church that day. Dark clouds floated outside the circle of windows. The loud whistle of the wind almost drowned out Amanda's soft voice.

"He didn't come to church today. I don't think he'll be back," Amanda said. "You know, I was fine before I ever met him, so why should it matter so much? He doesn't love me anymore, and that's that."

"I saw him storm out," Rose said. "He looked furious. And *hurt*. Look, what he was hearing from you was no more contact, period."

"But I was ready to follow him for the rest of my life," Amanda protested. "I was going to tell him . . . he didn't give me a chance!"

"He didn't know what your answer would be. As far as he knows, you never answered him at all," Lizabeth said.

"I think Jed does love you," Rose said. "I think his pride was wounded."

"The way your father disapproves of him—criminy, he even disapproves of Jed's letters! How do you think that makes him feel?" Kat said.

"It took a lot of courage for him to keep showing up in your father's church all this time," Rose said. "And all for a *glimpse* of you!"

"I don't know," Amanda said. "Do you *really* think he loves me?"

"What we think doesn't matter," Kat said. "You have to find out for sure. You have to go talk to him."

"But he left me standing there!"

"If it was only because he was hurt, you need to know that," Rose said. "If he's tired of waiting for you, you need to know that, too. You both ought to make everything clear."

Amanda looked out of the tower window. The sky was gray and the waves were crashing furiously against the rocks. There seemed to be a squall out at sea. She turned back and sighed. "How and where do I talk to him? I mean, if I even get up the nerve."

"For goodness' sake, Amanda!" Lizabeth said. "You know very well that he works on the *Mary Lee*. All you have to do is take a stroll along the docks."

"What if he won't talk to me at all? What if I ask him straight out and he says he's not interested anymore?" Amanda asked. "I don't think I could handle that."

"If that's the way it turns out," Kat said, "the four of us can get together and drown him!"

"Kat!" Amanda exclaimed.

Kat shook her head. "It would be just like you to throw him a life preserver!"

"Anything is better than pining away and not knowing," Lizabeth said. "And if it's a misunderstanding keeping you apart, well, that would be much too sad."

"The *Mary Lee* collects the lobster cages well before dawn and comes back to dock in the morning," Kat said.

"You should make a plan to go there," Rose said.

"Suppose you feel like taking a walk when you

wake up," Lizabeth said, "and your feet happen to carry you to Wharf Way."

Amanda took a breath. "I'll find him. I'll do it tomorrow morning. I *have* to know."

"Good girl!" Rose cheered. "Wait—do you need someone to take care of Hannah?"

"How could I forget! Yes, I do," Amanda said. "Father leaves at eight and I don't want to take her along, not for this."

"Then I'll come over around nine," Rose said. "Is that all right?"

"Thank you! I won't be long, I won't keep you from the stables and Midnight Star."

"Unless Jed tells you he loves you," Lizabeth said, grinning. "Then you might be *very* long!"

"No, honestly, I'll come straight back home."

"We'll keep our fingers crossed all morning," Kat said.

"How could he *not* love you? He's crazy if he doesn't," Rose said.

Amanda looked around at Kat, Lizabeth, and Rose. "You three! You're the best friends anyone could have."

They piled into a four-way bear hug. Whatever Jed says, however it turns out, Amanda thought, I'll still have my friends. She knew she was preparing herself for the worst.

It rained all night Sunday. By Monday morning it had stopped, but when Amanda looked out the front hall window, she saw streams of water still coursing along the sides of the path. The daylilies at the roadside had been flattened.

Rose burst into Amanda's house, clutching her jacket around her. "It's cold outside," she said, "and the trees are still dripping."

Amanda pulled her wool shawl from the coat tree. She was wearing her sturdy brown leather high-button boots. "Not my prettiest shoes," she said, "but I guess the most practical."

Rose nodded.

"Hannah's in her room with her paper dolls," Amanda said. "If you'll help her cut out the clothes, she'll be perfectly happy."

"Don't worry, we'll be fine."

"All right then, I'll be back soon. Thanks, Rose." Amanda hesitated with her hand on the doorknob. "It's not as though I'm meeting him behind my father's back, is it? I mean, it's not a *prearranged* meeting. We'll talk for only a minute."

"You're only taking a stroll along the docks. And if you happen to run into him . . ."

"Because I'm not a sneak," Amanda said.

"Don't worry, you're not. Go ahead, Amanda. And good luck!"

Outside the air was heavy and damp. Amanda wrapped her shawl tight around her shoulders as she carefully walked around the puddles on Lighthouse Lane. It's only August sixth, she thought, but it already feels like fall.

Her steps became slower as she approached the docks. What will I say? She had tossed on her sheets all night, trying to compose the right words. Her eyes felt sandy from lack of sleep. There's no sense in planning ahead, she thought. The look on his face when he sees me will tell me a lot. And if nothing else comes to me, I'll have to be bold enough to ask, "Were you angry for a minute or are we finished for good?" That's all I need to know.

The docks were bustling with activity. Boats were coming in and unloading the night's catch. Others were loading up, getting ready to set sail. Amanda made her way past men hauling barrels and pulling ropes, calling to each other: "Give me a hand there, Mike," "Watch out below!" "Easy does it."

Amanda spotted the *Mary Lee*. The berths on either side of her were vacant, left empty by ships out at sea.

Amanda checked the men swabbing the *Mary Lee*'s deck and others pulling full lobster cages from the hull. Jed wasn't among them. Amanda shivered and waited. She hoped to catch sight of Jed, but she dreaded it too. If he had lost interest, she would be horribly humiliated. Maybe she shouldn't have listened to her friends and come here.

A damp gray fog rolled in from the harbor. Amanda paced nervously in front of the *Mary Lee*. On deck, men were hoisting and hauling, pulling ropes and folding canvas, in some well-rehearsed tuneless dance. Jed could be working below. Should she ask for him? Was it terrible to interrupt him at his job? It would be so much better if she just casually bumped into him. But what was she *casually* doing at the docks? Finally, she made herself approach the nearest sailor.

"Excuse me, sir. I'd like to speak to Jed Langford, please."

The sailor didn't look up from the knot he was tying. "He's not here."

"Um, do you know where he is?" Amanda's eyes darted along the dock, to a group of men gulping coffee.

Jed wasn't with them. Was he having a quick breakfast somewhere else, or lunch, or whatever? "Is he coming back soon?"

"No. Jed Langford's gone."

eleven

"Gone?" Amanda echoed.

The sailor took a good look at her for the first time. "Jed left. He went up to New Bedford."

"*Jed Langford? Left?*" To New Bedford. To ship out! Without a word. "Are you sure?"

"Yeah, well, a couple of weeks back, I think," the sailor said.

Amanda felt all the blood draining from her face. She stared stupidly at the sailor.

"Listen, are you all right?"

She nodded. She was rooted to the spot.

"You want a drink of water or something?"

"No," Amanda murmured through numb lips. She pulled her shawl tight and hugged herself, shaking.

She wandered home along Lighthouse Lane, unaware of the puddles she splashed through. But Jed *must* have left a message for her! He couldn't—he *wouldn't* leave without a word!

She reversed direction and hurried toward the lighthouse. She rushed into the cave. There was nothing in the crevice. She felt along the moist walls with her heart hammering. She stepped further in. In the dim light, she looked in every crack of stone for a paper bag. There was nothing. Nothing.

Back onto Lighthouse Lane and in the direction of home. An automatic turn onto her front path. She twisted the doorknob. Hung her shawl on the coat tree. Removed her shoes on the hall mat so she wouldn't track mud on the wooden floor.

"Amanda? What's the matter?" Rose was next to her. "Did you talk to him?"

Amanda shook her head.

"What happened? What is it?"

"He's gone to New Bedford," Amanda wailed. "He must be on the high seas by now. He didn't even say good-bye. He didn't care at all!"

"I don't believe that. I really don't," Rose said.

"We only had that one evening. That barn dance, way back last October. I guess that was nothing. But I bared my soul to him in my letters. I thought I *knew* him.

How could I be so wrong, Rose?"

"There must be an explanation," Rose said.

Amanda shook her head. She took a breath and gathered herself. "Everything go all right with Hannah?"

Rose nodded. "We had fun."

"Thanks, Rose."

"Amanda, do you want me to stay?"

"Oh, no, I'm all right. And you have to get to the stables. I'm just so tired and chilled. I'm going to lie down for a little while."

Amanda lay on her bed with a quilt pulled up to her chin. Lines from Jed's letters went around and around in her mind. "I want to tuck you in my shirt pocket and take care of you." "I'll wait for you until the end of time 'cause there's nobody else I want to be with." She wished she could reread all his letters to decipher why it had all suddenly changed. They were *her* letters and *her* property! Father had no right to bully her into burning them!

She could hear Hannah in the next room, prattling in different voices, speaking for her paper dolls. Amanda was cold, so cold, and her bones felt impossibly heavy.

She dozed on and off. She drifted through strange dreams. All alone in a tiny boat. Huge, hulking gray shapes surrounding her, a Nantucket sleigh ride pulling her down, down to the mercilessly cold bottom of the sea. . . . She woke up, whispering, "Mama."

Often when she was sad, she felt her mother's presence watching over her. She needed her real flesh-and-blood mother now. She needed a woman to ask about her new womanly feelings. Mama, I miss you so much, she thought, now more than ever.

Amanda heard noises coming from downstairs in the kitchen. A metal spoon scraping against a pot. Hannah's voice. Father's voice. Mrs. Cornell, too—she was here again!

Amanda sat up. An enticing smell drifted from downstairs—frying pork? It had to be late afternoon already. She must have skipped lunch. Hannah must have managed to get something for herself, to let her sleep.

Amanda ran her hand through her hair, smoothed the wrinkles from her skirt as best she could, and headed for the stairs.

Halfway down, she could hear Mrs. Cornell say, "Now half a cup of flour."

And then Hannah piped up, "Yes, Mama."

Amanda flew down the rest of the stairs and burst into the kitchen. "Hannah! *What* did you say? *She's not your mother!*"

"I was just—just playing." Hannah, at the kitchen counter, was wide-eyed. She almost dropped the measuring cup in her hand. "Pretend make believe."

"Well, stop pretending! She's not your—" Amanda's eyes swept over Mrs. Cornell, standing next to Hannah. *What* was Mrs. Cornell holding? The recipe box!

Amanda roughly grabbed it out of her hand. "That's my mother's! In her own handwriting! You have no right!" This was too much, on top of everything else.

"Amanda!" Father was sitting at the kitchen table.

Amanda couldn't look at him. She concentrated on lining up the top edges of the worn recipe cards. She closed the box.

"I didn't realize," Mrs. Cornell said. "I saw the file and I thought I'd try something. . . . I never meant to—to intrude or—"

"*Why* are you making our dinner?" Amanda interrupted. "I'm perfectly capable of—"

"I know you are," Mrs. Cornell said. "I planned to invite all of you to my place tonight, but you won't believe what a tiny kitchen I have. I thought it would be easier to put something together here. I'm sorry if . . . I didn't know."

"You owe Mrs. Cornell an apology," Father said.

Amanda set her lips in a grim line. Didn't anyone care that this woman was shoving both her and her mother aside?

"Let it go, Roger. Please," Mrs. Cornell said.

That's Reverend Morgan to *you*, Amanda thought.

"We're making gingerbreaded pork chops," Hannah said brightly. "I helped with all the measuring and mixing."

Gingerbreaded pork chops? That didn't sound at all familiar. Had her mother ever actually made that or had she collected the recipe for later? Amanda couldn't remember. It hurt to think that her mother was disappearing in the fog of memory.

"I'm waiting to hear your apology," Father said.

Amanda wasn't sorry for anything she'd said! How dare Mrs. Cornell put her flour-smeared hands all over her mother's things!

Father stared at her.

"I'm sorry I yelled," Amanda finally forced out.

"It's forgotten." Mrs. Cornell kept busy dipping chops in flour, then beaten egg, and then breading. Some were already sizzling in the frying pan.

Father wasn't satisfied. "I didn't raise you to be rude, Amanda."

Amanda whirled around to face him. "You didn't raise me at all! I raised myself!"

Father glared at her. "What is that supposed to mean?"

Her misery and anger had made her go too far. "Nothing," she mumbled.

Mrs. Cornell kept her concentration on the stove. Her back looked stiff.

The ticking of the grandfather clock in the hall seemed especially loud.

Mrs. Cornell turned and cleared her throat. "Amanda, if you and Hannah could set the table, please. We're almost ready."

Mrs. Cornell, the peacemaker! Why couldn't she mind her own business?

Hannah bounced around the table, placing napkins. Amanda followed her, putting down the silverware with angry thumps.

They sat down to dinner. A cloud of tension hung over the table. Father gave Amanda outraged looks. She knew he wanted to reprimand her, but not in front of Mrs. Cornell.

Mrs. Cornell tried to make conversation. Soon she gave up. Even Hannah was quiet. She looked, puzzled, from one strained face to another.

Gingerbreaded pork chops, mashed potatoes, and salad. It was a good meal, but Amanda couldn't bring herself to come up with a compliment. She chewed automatically and could barely swallow.

For a long, awkward time, the only sounds at the table were forks and knives scraping against plates. Mrs. Cornell excused herself early and Father left to see her home.

When he comes back, Amanda thought, I'll get a lecture. She dreaded his disappointed looks and his low, cutting voice.

Well, she'd face it later. First, she had to draw Hannah's bath.

Hannah didn't want to play with her little yellow duck tonight. "Are you mad at me?" she asked.

Amanda sat on the edge of the tub and sighed as she ran a washcloth over Hannah's back. She was mad at the whole world tonight, but certainly not at her little sister. "No, pumpkin, not at you." She pushed a strand of wet hair back from Hannah's forehead. "You're very, *very* good. Rose said she had fun with you this morning."

"I like Rose," Hannah said. She hesitated. "I like Mrs. Cornell." She watched for Amanda's reaction.

"All right."

"I *know* she's not my mama, that was pretend, but . . ."

"But what?"

Hannah shrugged her narrow, soapy shoulders.

"Your mama's name was Teresa Lassiter Morgan."

"I know that. Teresa Lassiter Morgan," Hannah repeated.

"She was kind and gentle, and she loved us very much. We mustn't forget about her. She watches over us, Hannah, wherever we are."

"I know. You told me." Hannah's little face was troubled.

"What is it?"

"She never met me. Are you sure she watches over me, too?"

"Oh, yes, I'm sure."

"If Mrs. Cornell was somebody's mama—I know she's not—but if she *was*, she'd be a nice one."

"Maybe," Amanda said. It was painful to see Hannah's longing.

It was close to midnight when Amanda heard Father come in. She heard him moving around in his study. He didn't call her downstairs. That was a relief for now, but she knew he'd have a lot to say in the morning.

~twelve~

The next morning Amanda was the first in the kitchen.

She stirred eggs, milk, cinnamon, and flour together in a mixing bowl. Yesterday she had allowed her misery and anger to overwhelm her. She desperately wanted everything to be back to normal with Father. She could at least make an especially nice breakfast of flapjacks for him.

She dropped spoonfuls of batter on the hot griddle. Oh, it was sizzling too fast! Amanda turned the heat down. The stove was hard to control. The first batch burned around the edges and remained soft and runny in the center. But she had to cook them through, didn't she? By the time the center was solid, the edges were black. She piled them on the serving platter and covered it with another dish to keep warm. I'll eat the bad ones, she thought. Anyway, there's fresh maple syrup in the pantry and the sweetness will cover the burned flavor.

Amanda opened the window to air out the bitter smell. The weather had turned. It was bright and sunny, a perfect summer day; it made her feel hopeful.

She was carefully flipping the next batch of flapjacks when Father came into the kitchen. The buoyant bounce he'd had in his step lately was gone.

"Good morning, Father," Amanda said cautiously.

"Morning." He didn't look at her as he sat down at the table. His face was especially thin and etched with tired lines, as if he'd aged overnight. His shoulders were stooped. I guess he didn't sleep well last night either, Amanda thought.

She served him a plate of flapjacks from the new batch. The edges were still browner and crisper than they should have been.

"They're a tiny bit burned," Amanda said nervously, "but with loads of maple syrup . . ."

He began to eat without a glance at her.

"Are they good? I tried my best." She was hovering around him too anxiously. "I added cinnamon. The stove gets hot too quickly and—"

"They're all right." Father looked directly at her for the first time. "Are we going to talk about flapjacks now?"

"Um . . . no. Not if you don't want to."

"Sit down, Amanda."

"Yes, Father."

"You've effectively driven Doris Cornell away. I think you should know that. If that's what you intended, I don't understand why."

"I didn't intend anything. But she was wrong to go through Mama's things." Amanda paused and explained, "I guess it . . . it made me mad."

"There wasn't a label on the recipe box saying 'hands off, this belonged to Teresa Morgan.' It looks like any ordinary recipe file. How could Doris possibly know it would upset you?"

"All right." Amanda tried to be agreeable. "I didn't stop to think."

"You were inexcusably rude to a guest in our house. And the way you screamed at your sister! I was ashamed of you."

Amanda colored.

"Doris is the best thing that's happened to Hannah. Her warmth and generosity—I would think you'd appreciate that."

Amanda's eyes widened. "The *best* thing? She hasn't exactly taken care of her all these years!"

"You know that's not what I meant, Amanda. Just that she enjoyed being with Hannah, and Hannah felt it. Doris is playful and—"

"She can play with Hannah all she wants," Amanda mumbled.

"No, Doris won't be back." Father pushed away his plate. He looked as sad as Amanda had ever seen him. "She has no interest in becoming the evil stepmother. She doesn't want to be responsible for problems in our family."

"*What?* What do you mean, *stepmother*?"

"I had asked Doris for her hand. Last night, she turned me down. She said she can't and won't fight your hostility. It wasn't only yesterday, it was—"

"Her hand in *marriage*?" Amanda was stunned. "How *could* you? You hardly know her!"

"We've been friendly for a long time. We've chatted at the bookshop; she's been involved in church activities." His eyes dropped and he seemed to be concentrating on the tines of his fork. Amanda was astonished. He seemed almost awkward and shy, and she was touched in spite of herself. "It took Miranda Forbes to give us that extra nudge. To make me realize it was still possible."

"It's much too fast!"

"Sometimes you know when it's right." Father's eyes met hers and she was moved by the emotion she saw welling up in them.

He seemed so terribly lost. He'd been lonely for so long.

Amanda loved him, and if Mrs. Cornell could make it better for him . . . But that night at the barn dance, Amanda had known Jed Langford was right for her, too, and Father had refused to listen and now it was all spoiled!

Amanda hardened her heart. "I felt the same way about Jed Langford . . . I would never be that disrespectful of *your* feelings."

Father waved his hand dismissively. "You're still a child, Amanda."

"I'm not! I live here and I take care of everything in this house, and I should have been allowed to invite a friend . . . if I'm more than a serving girl around here!"

"You're being a bit dramatic, aren't you?" Father said. "As a matter of fact, Doris sided with you. She said I should allow a few visits, under supervision, of course. Though I think that boy is entirely unsuitable."

"You talked to Mrs. Cornell about me?" That was the worst betrayal of all.

Father nodded. "I trust her."

"But you told her my personal, private—"

"Everyone in church knows about you and that boy. They've all seen your antics."

Without shouting, in his calm, controlled manner he could make her feel small and ashamed. But she hadn't meant to do anything wrong! She tried so hard to do everything right.

"You could make far better use of your time than mooning over him," he continued.

"*Better use of my time?*" Something snapped inside Amanda. "I keep up the house, I take care of Hannah, don't you even notice? I have no time! You can't call me a child and then heap all the responsibilities on me!"

"Amanda, settle down. What is this about? We do have the laundress and the cleaning girl once a week."

"You should at least *know* what has to be done! Someone has to sort the laundry and tell the cleaning girl what to do and shop and cook and make sure Hannah's clean and dressed right and—" Amanda was suddenly breathless, with everything spilling out. "And—and when school is in session and there's homework . . . I don't have time to breathe! I don't mind helping, but I try so hard to please you and make you proud, and you don't even notice! I'll never be perfect enough to win your respect. I was up early this morning to make you flapjacks. I try so hard—"

"You're not making sense, Amanda. Oatmeal or toast would have been fine."

"You only notice when something goes wrong. You don't even see me or Hannah, not really!" It all poured out in a confused jumble, things that she hadn't even admitted to herself. "You're hardly ever home; you're never here with us. I know you do good works and help everyone, but do you have to run to Mrs. Malloy every time she has a hangnail and—"

"Mrs. Malloy is a helpless, lonely old woman," Father interrupted. "Her children live out of state and neglect her."

"*We're* lonely and neglected! When was the last time you read a bedtime story to Hannah? I knew you were grieving, I knew keeping busy helped you. I understood all that. But then Mrs. Cornell came along and suddenly you have all the time in the world for her and— It's nice that you go to the orphanage to check on the children there, and everyone says you're a great man, but—but we're almost orphans right here. All we get is the crumbs! I *want* to take care of Hannah, I love her, but I can't do it without your help!"

Father looked surprised and a little uncertain. "Hannah is perfectly all right."

"Hannah needs a grown-up parent—she called a strange woman mama! And maybe I want someone to take care of *me* for a change! At least sometimes. Someone to pay attention!"

Amanda stopped, out of breath. She was shocked by all that had spilled out from her. Father, across the table, seemed shaken. The air between them trembled in the silence. Amanda thought, Father might open his arms to me now, I'll rush into them, and we'll forgive and comfort each other.

There were footsteps on the staircase. And then Hannah's voice. "I heard you say my name."

Hannah appeared in the kitchen, hugging her teddy bear under one arm.

"Um . . . yes. Breakfast," Amanda said. "I kept some flapjacks warm for you."

Hannah sat down at the table next to Father. Her feet wound around the bottom rungs of the chair. She held up her teddy bear and giggled. "Say hello to Mr. Snippydoodle."

Amanda picked out the less-burned flapjacks and served Hannah. "I thought his name was Billy T. Bear."

"Not anymore. When Rose was here, we made up funny names for all my animals." She giggled again. "My pink rabbit is Miss Hoppingcotton!"

Father glanced at Amanda and then focused on Hannah. "That *is* a funny name." He smiled.

Amanda went to the icebox for milk. He's trying, she thought.

Hannah basked in his attention. She began to prattle away to hold his interest. "Rose came to take care of me when Amanda went away and she knows lots of funny names and we cut out paper dolls and—"

"When was that?" Father asked.

"Yesterday morning," Hannah said. And, proudly showing off her knowledge, "Monday morning, August sixth, 1906. And the ground was all yucky from the rain and so we couldn't play outside and—"

Father's attention slid away from Hannah. "Where did you go, Amanda?"

Amanda faced him, with her back to the icebox and the bottle of milk in her hand. There were many things she could say that would satisfy him, she thought. Any errand. To the bakery. To the post office. She didn't want to take Hannah along because it was so wet.

The pause had become too long. Father was watching her, no longer casual.

I'm not going to lie, Amanda thought. Why should I lie when I did nothing wrong! Maybe now we can finally talk to each other.

She straightened her shoulders. "I went to the docks. I was back home in less than an hour."

"Why the docks?" Father asked.

Amanda scraped up her courage. I'm not a liar. I'm not a child and I don't want to feel ashamed. "To find Jed Langford. I needed to ask him something."

"*What?* You went to meet him in some out-of-the-way corner? Though you were forbidden?"

"It wasn't like that," Amanda said quickly. "It wasn't *meeting*, it was . . ."

Amanda's voice trailed off. Father's face had become an icy mask. With a sinking feeling she realized she'd made a mistake.

"Sneaking around when I'm not home . . . And you think I should *respect* you?" He was using her words against her! "What have you turned into, Amanda? A deceitful—"

"No, I'm not—" Amanda protested.

"And that boy put you up to it! I knew he was trouble from the beginning. You're to keep away—"

"It doesn't matter! Jed Langford's gone. He's *gone!*"

Amanda was suddenly trembling with fury. "I'm going to Kat's. And I'm staying over. Mrs. Williams will welcome me!" She ran to the kitchen door and then she whirled around to face Father again. "Mary Margaret is coming over to play with Hannah and *you* can take care of them! Oh, and you'd better braid her hair so it won't tangle. *You* can get lunch together . . . you should know we're out of bread. Oh, and the chimney sweep's due this afternoon. You can clean up after him!"

Amanda ran out of the house and along Lighthouse Lane. The bright sunlight shimmered in her tears and almost blinded her. Kat's cottage and the lighthouse at Durham Point were her haven. During that awful first year, when Great-aunt Myrtle was grudgingly taking care of them, Amanda spent every possible minute she could at Kat's.

Just before she turned onto the path to the cottage, Amanda slowed to a walk and wiped away her tears. Even if Kat isn't home right now, she thought, this is the one place where I'm always accepted. Kat's mother and father were the warmest, most generous people she could imagine.

There was Mr. Williams now, coming out of the

cottage and heading toward the lighthouse with the energetic stride that almost hid his limp. Amanda stopped short. He was carrying a huge butcher knife. Sunlight glinted on the wide steel blade.

⊱*thirteen*⊰

"Hello, Mr. Williams!" Amanda called.

"Morning, Amanda." He stopped on the path and waited for her to catch up. He seemed cheerful and relaxed, so the big butcher's knife in his hand wasn't about an emergency, Amanda thought. She was relieved; everything was all right.

In the sun, his auburn hair, exactly like Kat's, looked fiery. He was a big, well-muscled man with an easy smile. Just being in his presence made Amanda feel comfortable and protected.

"What's happening?" Amanda asked.

"You mean this?" He indicated the sharp steel blade in his hand. "We've received a gift from the sea."

"A gift from the sea?" All Amanda could think of was pearls and mermaids.

"Come on along. Kat and Lizabeth are down at the beach."

Amanda followed Mr. Williams along the path and around the corner past the lighthouse. She blinked. Two huge black shapes were at the water's edge: well, one huge and the other a great deal smaller, covering an enormous area of sand. What in the world. . . . She stopped, hesitant to come close.

"Amanda, look what turned up," Kat called.

"It's so sad," Lizabeth said.

At the same time, grizzled old Jeremiah Baxter from Wharf Way waded out of the sea and threw a bucket of seawater on the huge shapes. "Help me!" he pleaded. "Somebody, please, fill another bucket!"

"Look, Jeremiah, I'm going to harvest—" Mr. Williams began.

"No, Tom! Give them a chance." Mr. Baxter's gray beard didn't cover the deep lines on his raw, weather-beaten face. He was heavy-set and solidly balanced on powerful legs. "At least wait until high tide!" He turned and hurried back to the water to refill his bucket.

Whales! Beached whales! The small one was huddled next to the big one. The big one's fin seemed to move a bit, touching, stroking, the small one. Amanda's breath caught. *A mother and her baby!* Mrs. Cornell's words, words that she had barely listened to, came back to her. "Carries the baby for sixteen months . . . mammals . . . nurse their young . . . calves often stay alongside long after they're weaned. . . ." Only the very tip of the mother's tail was in the water.

A mother and her baby, beached and dying on the sand! And no one but Mr. Baxter was doing anything!

"They're pilot whales," Kat said. "That's the smallest kind, but still—the big one has to be sixteen feet!"

Mr. Baxter had run back and poured more water over the mother's skin. There wasn't enough to cover all of it. There wasn't enough water left for the baby. He made a quick, frantic turn back to the sea and this time, Amanda ran after him.

"I'll help!" she shouted. "What, where—"

She spotted another bucket at the water's edge and filled it with seawater. It was heavy and some water splashed out as she ran to the whales.

"Careful," Mr. Baxter gasped. "Don't pour on the blowhole. They breathe air through it; you could drown them."

Amanda poured her water on the baby, avoiding the blowhole, and she rushed back for more.

"Got to keep them cool and wet," Mr. Baxter said as he passed her on yet another run with a full bucket.

It seemed like a spoonful of water at a time, hardly covering their glistening black skins.

The sun was bright in the sky.

"Kat! Lizabeth! Help me!" Amanda called desperately. "Kat!"

"I don't know," Kat said slowly. She looked up at her father.

It suddenly hit Amanda. Mr. Williams, a man she loved almost as much as her own father, was going to cut up the whales! That's what the knife was for. That's what he meant by "harvesting"!

"Give them a chance, Mr. Williams," she begged, echoing Mr. Baxter. "Until high tide."

"Look, it's a waste of—" Mr. Williams was stopped by the despair on Amanda's face. He shrugged. "All right, there's no rush—I'll wait a little while. Only for you, Amanda. But high tide won't help. You'll never get eighteen hundred pounds back to sea. Jeremiah's an old fool."

Amanda ran to fill yet another bucket. Mr. Williams was a whaler before he was the lighthouse keeper, she thought. He had hunted and killed whales; that's what whalers did! And Kat, her best friend, was his daughter and idolized her father. But didn't Kat see—didn't they all see—here was a mother and her baby!

A dying mother! She *had* to save her! She and Mr. Baxter couldn't do it alone. "Kat! Lizabeth! Please!"

"Amanda's asking for our help and that's good enough for me." Lizabeth said. "Come on, Kat!" She joined the bucket brigade and then Kat did, too.

That gave Mr. Baxter a chance to catch his breath for a moment. "We should soak some towels. To help cool them and prevent sunburn."

More buckets. Amanda, Mr. Baxter, Lizabeth, and Kat, over and over again, brought full buckets to the whales, empty buckets back to the sea. Both whales were breathing. Amanda could see it. Faint and labored, but breathing. There *had* to be hope!

Amanda's arms ached. Sweat ran from her forehead and into her eyes. The relentless sun shimmered in the sky. She lost all track of time. Minutes and hours passed, measured in more and more buckets. Through blurred vision, she saw that a crowd had gathered. The news had spread through Cape Light.

There were men standing by with knives and axes. Women were chatting and casually observing the scene. A weekday morning, and all these people had turned out, waiting for the big event!

"Please help!" Amanda shouted.

She wasn't aware that tears were streaming down her face. A few people stepped back. But most of them stared at Amanda, honestly puzzled.

"Amanda. Amanda, I'm here." It was Rose. Thank goodness, Amanda thought. Rose, who had saved an abused horse, would understand more than anyone. "What should I do?"

"Buckets. More buckets," Amanda gasped. "We have to keep them cool. Have to keep them wet."

Suddenly Mrs. Cornell appeared out of nowhere. She was alongside the whales, holding soaking wet towels and flour sacks in both arms, and listening to Mr. Baxter.

"Cover all the exposed areas. Not the blowhole," he warned. "And not the fins. They help lose heat from the body."

Mrs. Cornell nodded and followed his instructions.

Another trip. The mother whale's eyes looked cloudy to Amanda. Was she imagining that they were somehow huddling closer? The mother protecting the baby as best she could with her body? No, they were unable to move on the sand, but Amanda *felt* their bond. And their terror. She felt herself nuzzling close to her dying mother. . . . No, she knew imagination was getting the best of her, but she couldn't stop sobbing.

"All right, Jeremiah, enough of this," Mr. White called. "We want to get to work."

"Give me until high tide," Mr. Baxter pleaded.

The whales were still breathing. It was very faint, but Amanda could see. They were still breathing!

"Nonsense, Jeremiah!" Now Mr. Thomas was angry. "You have more scrimshaw than anybody! Now get those girls out of the way."

They were such a small band, Amanda thought. Kat, Lizabeth, Rose, Mrs. Cornell, Mr. Baxter, and herself trying to buy more time and give the whales a chance. Again, she turned to Kat's father. "Please, Mr. Williams," she begged. "Give us time."

Mr. Williams glanced at Amanda's tear-stained face. Then he spoke to the crowd in his usual easygoing and jovial manner. "All right, I'm with you on this, you know that, but high tide will be around five, only a little while longer. So let's indulge the tender feelings of my daughter and her friends for a bit."

"We need daylight to see what we're doing," someone grumbled.

"Come on, Joe, there's still plenty of daylight at five," Mr. Williams said. "And why work in the heat of the day?"

Mr. Williams was a man who was well respected in Cape Light. They wouldn't have paid attention to anyone else, Amanda thought.

More buckets. Towels removed, resoaked, and put back. Amanda was working alongside Mrs. Cornell. She hesitated for a moment and then said, "Thanks. For helping."

"There's no need to thank me," Mrs. Cornell said. "I'm doing it for the whales. I came down as soon as I heard. . . . I had no idea you'd be here or even interested."

"Anyway, I'm glad you're helping," Amanda said.

"All right," Mrs. Cornell said. "Maybe, surprisingly enough, we do have something in common."

Amanda pushed back her hair. "If I was rude the other day," she said. "I wasn't that mad at you. I was mostly mad at my father."

"Well, that's something for your family to sort out, isn't it?" Mrs. Cornell turned to carry another empty bucket to the sea.

The sun sank lower in the sky. Amanda watched the shoreline. The water was lapping up a little farther on the mother's tail. More buckets. Amanda's arms felt torn out of their sockets. If she didn't care so much, if she wasn't so desperate, she would have been mortified to be struggling so frantically in front of the indifferent and restless crowd. Amanda had never found herself on the unpopular side before.

Now the water was edging along the baby's tail. And—thank you, God!—inching higher.

After a long while, Mr. Baxter said, "High tide. This is their chance."

The water had risen enough to cover more than half of the baby's body. Its tail flipped a little in the shallows. Otherwise, it didn't move.

"We've got to help it along with a push," Mr. Baxter said. "If we can. We'll have to take a chance on scraping its skin on the sand."

Their little band surrounded the smaller whale. Amanda's hands touched the surprisingly warm, glistening black body. She tried to find a good hold.

"One, two, go!" Mr. Baxter said.

Nothing happened.

Again, "One, two, go!" Amanda saw the veins stand out in Mr. Baxter's forehead and Mrs. Cornell's determined clenched jaw. She felt the tremendous strain in her arms.

Nothing.

"Come on, baby," Mr. Baxter said. "Everybody, take a breath and try again. One, two, GO!"

They were all red-faced with strain. Maybe it was their great united effort, maybe it was a wave that lapped higher at just that very moment— The baby was in the water! The baby was completely in the water! And swimming!

The girls started to cheer, but they stopped almost immediately. The baby was swimming, but not far enough from the shoreline. It was circling and in danger of beaching itself again. It was trying to return to its mother!

"Come on, quick!" Mr. Baxter went into the water and set up a commotion, stamping his feet, knocking tin buckets against the rocks. The others followed his example. The enormous clamor they created made some of the crowd on shore laugh, but the baby whale was finally terrorized enough to swim out to sea.

"Now the mother! We have to save the mother!" Amanda said.

Mr. Baxter put his hand on her shoulder. "The water never came high enough for her."

"But . . . the *mother*!" Amanda cried.

"We tried," Mr. Baxter said sadly. "We did our best. We needed high tide to cover most of her body, and it didn't. It just wasn't enough."

"Please, we have to try—"

"There's nothing left to do," Mr. Baxter said. "It's time to give up."

"No! No!" Amanda screamed.

Now Mr. Williams's arm was around her. "Come on, Amanda. Come into the cottage now with the rest of the girls."

"Not yet," Amanda moaned.

"I don't want you to see," Mr. Williams said.

"I won't look," Amanda sobbed. She turned to Kat, Lizabeth, and Rose. "I'll be there in a little while. I can't leave yet. I can't."

Kat took her hand and whispered. "Come inside with us."

"In a minute, but—" Amanda said. "I want to watch for the baby. I have to."

Mr. Baxter nodded. "I'll go with her."

He led her to the rocks below the lighthouse, well out of sight of the crowd and the mother whale. Amanda heard something ripping and then the grunts of men hard at work. She shuddered. Mr. Baxter led her farther along the rocky shore, where the roar of the ocean covered the terrible sounds. But they were still echoing in her ears.

Mr. Baxter gave her a sympathetic look. "We saved the baby. You got the other girls to help, and convinced Mr. Williams to wait until high tide. That surely made the difference."

"And Mrs. Cornell helped, too," Amanda admitted.

"Yes, well, Doris Cornell, with all the reading she does . . . She thinks differently from anyone else in this town." He chuckled. "She's her own person, all right."

They climbed up on a rock and found a ledge to sit on, out of the spray. Amanda looked out to sea, squinting, scanning the horizon for water spouting into the air.

"No sign of the baby," she said. "I don't see anything at all."

"That means it kept going away from shore," Mr. Baxter said.

"Does it have a chance all by itself?"

"I don't know," Mr. Baxter said. "I hope it was weaned. It looked old enough to feed by itself. I hope it can find its pod."

"How do you know so much about whales?" Amanda asked. "You knew exactly what to do."

Mr. Baxter sighed. "Oh, I know about whales. Right whales, sperm whales, humpback, you name it. I spent a good part of my life hunting them, from New England to the South Seas. Jeremiah Baxter was well known as one of the best."

Amanda was shocked. "Is that what Mr. Thomas meant when he said you had more scrimshaw than anyone?"

Mr. Baxter nodded. "I went for the oil, but I collected the ivory, too. Oh, I was good at it. To hunt them down efficiently, I studied them. I learned their behavior and their habits. And the more I learned, the more my mind opened up to what they really are. Sensitive, intelligent, feeling beings, attached to their pods, attached to their young. Gentle and magnificent. And I just couldn't do it anymore." He sighed. "If I save one beached whale, that doesn't make up for the hundreds I've harpooned. It was bloody slaughter on the high seas."

Amanda looked out at the beautiful, indifferent sea. She sent up a prayer for the baby whale, for all babies and mothers, for everything defenseless and hunted. Oh, please keep the baby safe from whalers. . . . Even people like Jed Langford!

"I try to atone any way I can," Mr. Baxter went on. "Which puts me out of step with the fishing folk of Cape Light. Most of the town thinks I'm a half-wit."

Jed Langford had written constantly about whaling,

the price of whale oil, harpooning . . . Where had her mind been? How could she have been so blissfully thoughtless about what it meant? It took actually *seeing* the whales to make her aware.

There was no need to think about Jed now, though. He was gone. It was over. And yet, some part of her wanted to tell him about this day and her pained feelings. She had to find a way to wipe him out of her mind.

fourteen

Lizabeth and Rose went home before dark. Amanda was glad to stay over at Kat's, especially after the scene at breakfast this morning. The Williamses made her welcome, as Amanda knew they would.

They had just finished dinner and Amanda looked at their warm, familiar faces around the table. She loved them all; she'd loved them since she was a little girl, but—Mr. Williams had been one of those harvesting the beached whale today! He'd seemed cruelly indifferent.

And yet their big white dog Sunshine had the most attentive home any animal could want. The same went for their horse Dobbins. At this very moment, little Jamie was outside playing with Sunshine.

Mr. Williams pushed away the remains of his rice pudding and continued the conversation about the day's events. Amanda had tried to keep her end of it politely neutral, but he had picked up on her seething feelings.

"Don't be so angry, Amanda," he said. "This is a sea-faring town. Almost all the people here live from the sea."

"Cape Light people are truly kind and good," Mrs. Williams put in. "You know that, dear."

"I always thought so," Amanda said, "but now . . . Some of them were *mocking* Jeremiah Baxter!"

"A lot of people think he's a fanatic," Kat said. "They lose patience with him."

"He's not!" Amanda answered. "He's most certainly not!"

"I was just saying what some people think," Kat said. "I like him well enough."

"Amanda, what good would it do to leave the carcass rotting on the beach?" Mr. Williams asked.

"It was still alive! And none of those people even wanted to save it!"

"Every bit of that whale was put to use. It'll put food on a lot of tables. And it's possible that it beached itself because it was ill anyway."

"Do you think that's why?" Amanda asked.

"I don't know," Mr. Williams said. "It's one of the mysteries. Sometimes something goes wrong with their directional signals. Something separated those two from their pod. We'll never know." He shrugged. "I suppose I did feel sorry for them."

Amanda couldn't hold it back. "But you worked on a whaler and you didn't mind!"

"I liked the adventure of it. Until my leg got mangled and I couldn't manage a slippery deck anymore," Mr. Williams said. "There is killing in this world, Amanda, for food and other things that people need. Whether it's lobster cages or digging clams or whale oil . . . That's the way it is and I won't feel guilty about it."

"Maybe we should talk about something else," Mrs. Williams said.

"Wait, I want Amanda to know," Mr. Williams continued. "I do draw the line: I would never kill for fun or for pleasure."

"Well, my goodness, who would?" Kat said.

"Our president, for one," Mr. Williams said. "I hear the walls of Teddy Roosevelt's home at Sagamore Hill are covered with mounted heads of lions, tigers, bears, antelopes, zebras, whatever—all the animals he's proudly shot. Certainly not for any useful reason I can imagine. Now to my mind, that's an ugly waste. Still, I think he's a great president. He's done well for this country and I'll vote for him again."

"His children have loads of pets in the White House," Todd said. "I bet they're nice to them."

"I'm sure they are," Mrs. Williams agreed.

"Teddy bears are named after the president," Kat said. "Isn't that because he saved a bear cub once or something like that?"

"I don't know. That sounds like a nice story some-one made up." Mr. Williams turned to Amanda. "People are contradictory and not always on the side of the angels. I think you have to pick your battles. You have to decide for yourself what you can tolerate and what you won't accept at all."

"Anyway," Todd said, "whales aren't like puppies or kittens."

"Because they're not little and furry? What differ-ence does that make?" Amanda said. She knew Todd was especially smart and she was disappointed in him.

Before Todd could answer, Jamie came running in with Sunshine at his heels. "Amanda! Amanda! Your father's outside with the horse and carriage."

"He is?" Amanda turned to Mrs. Williams. "I told him I was staying over. I don't know why—"

"I suppose he wants you home tonight," Mrs. Williams said.

"I guess, but . . . I didn't expect him to pick me up."

Amanda thanked the Williamses, said her good-byes, and reluctantly headed for the cottage door.

Amanda and Father sat side by side in the carriage. Father hardly had to guide the horse. It knew the way as well as they did.

"I told you I was staying over at Kat's," Amanda said.

"I know. I wanted to get you." He cleared his throat. "I hope you don't mind too much."

"I guess it's all right." They were being artificially polite, Amanda thought. She was glad the darkness hid their expressions.

"After you left this morning," Father said, "I thought long and hard."

Only this morning? With everything that happened, it seemed as if much more than a day had gone by since their argument. Amanda was suddenly too exhausted to figure out if she was supposed to apologize now.

"If I've neglected you and Hannah—"

"I shouldn't have said that," Amanda interrupted.

"No, I can see the truth in it. It was never intentional. *I* know how deep my love for you is. I'm more sure of that than anything else in life. I suppose I thought you would know without my saying it, or showing it. That's always a mistake, isn't it? But you seemed perfectly fine—you both have friends, you both do well in school. . . ."

"I didn't mean that we were in some kind of terrible trouble," Amanda said, "only that we have so little of you. But that's all right. I know you have a lot to do."

"Don't smooth it over, Amanda. You do that often, you know. Your anger this morning was truthful." He cleared his throat. "I'm trying to say this right and I'm not sure if I can. I was almost going to write down my thoughts, the way I would a sermon. But . . . well, you can't present your daughter with an essay, can you?"

He's such a reserved, private man, Amanda thought. His discomfort was catching.

"I've thought about this all day. I was shattered when your mother died. I think I cut off my feelings at first, made myself numb, so the pain of it wouldn't tear me apart. Maybe that cut me off from my daughters, too. And I grew up with brothers and boy cousins. I didn't know anything about raising girls, so I suppose I had a lot of fear . . . But don't ever doubt my love for both of you."

"All right," Amanda said.

"I threw myself into good deeds and helping others until I was too exhausted to think about my grief. That wasn't the worst way of handling it at first, but I kept up the busyness for far too long. It was never deliberate, but over time I became used to it. I never intended to neglect you and Hannah."

That had to be so hard for him to say, Amanda thought.

He had let the reins go completely slack. The horse had stopped in the road and was contentedly munching the grass on the side.

"Father?" Amanda giggled nervously. "I just noticed. We're not going anywhere."

"What? Oh, you're right! Giddyap!" Father smiled. "That's what happens when you don't pay attention."

The carriage rolled on along Lighthouse Lane. A back wheel squeaked as usual.

"I have to get that oiled," Father muttered.

"You always say that."

"And never get around to it, do I?"

"No."

The chirping of the crickets in the underbrush along the lane was especially loud.

"I'm sorry if I was rude this morning," Amanda said.

"There were things you had to tell me. Amanda, I can see you're too burdened by household duties. I didn't realize. You should have spoken up sooner. What should we do? Would it help to have the cleaning girl come *twice* a week?"

"No, not really, and we can't afford it," Amanda said. "Honestly, I don't mind it most of the time. I wanted your appreciation, that's all. I wanted you to notice."

"You have my appreciation and my thanks. . . . Amanda, wouldn't another woman in the house make it easier for you?"

"Is this about Mrs. Cornell? Is *that* what it's about?" Amanda felt her resentment rise. "Mrs. Cornell happened too fast!"

Father nodded. "I know it's fast, but Doris and I have both suffered great losses. We've both struggled to go on. . . . When the bookstore was still the downstairs of a regular house, there were lots of bedrooms, Doris says, and she and Dan Cornell would look into them together and dream about filling them with boys and girls, noise and laughter. . . . That's so terribly sad, isn't it?"

"I'm sorry, but—"

"Amanda, like a wonderful, surprise gift, we were

given a second chance at happiness. That's something you grab with both hands!"

Amanda glanced sideways at him. "And all that new happiness wipes out your 'great loss'?"

"How can you think that? I loved your mother. Her name alone reminds me of everything beautiful and generous and graceful. Teresa. A contagious laugh, long dark hair, and the scent of violets . . . Even now, when I hear someone call out 'Teresa,' I stop in my tracks and my blood starts pumping though I realize it's only someone calling for a daughter or a friend. I *loved* her. Can't you see? That makes me open to loving again."

They rode along silently for a while. The horse's hooves beat a slow, rhythmic clip-clop.

"Couldn't you accept Doris?" Father asked. "Into our family?"

He sounded so suddenly unsure, almost shy, that Amanda ached for him. But a strange woman living with them, with her own ways, her own set of rules; bossing her, taking over and invading her privacy—it would be awful. And if Doris Cornell wanted to revive that dream of hers of filling bedrooms with babies—that could be a nightmare!

"She seems like a nice person. I don't have anything against Mrs. Cornell," Amanda said truthfully. "Can't you just keep company with her? Does it have to be *marriage*, with her coming into our *house*?"

"Yes it does. Can you accept that?"

"I don't know."

"What does that mean?" Father asked.

"It means I don't think so." Amanda bit her lip. "I'm sorry, I'm too used to being on my own. It would be . . . uncomfortable. For everybody, I think."

Father sighed a long, weary sigh. "All right. You were honest."

He sounded so defeated. "I don't want to hurt you. Maybe I need time to get used to the idea," Amanda said. She had to steel herself before she crumpled completely. "But, you know, you hurt *me*! You wouldn't listen to me at all about Jed. You refused to hear me."

"I wanted to talk about that, too," Father said. "I know you were angry that I spoke to Doris about the situation. You know, I can be very wise when it comes to counseling others, but it's not so easy to counsel myself. Everyone needs a confidante sometimes. Doris agreed that thirteen was too young, but—"

"Do I really need to hear what she thinks?"

"Yes. Please, let me finish. But she thought I was too strict and too protective. Mostly because I'm raising you all alone, without your mother's advice, and I don't always know what to do. I think Doris got it right. Sometimes I'm panicked by the huge responsibility for two little lives. Can you understand that?"

"I suppose."

"Doris said I should have allowed you to invite whomever you wanted, chaperoned of course, and—"

"That's all I asked for!"

"She said I had to trust you to behave properly. I had to have faith in you. Of course, Doris has no idea what a sweet, gentle soul you are. . . . Well, I brushed off her advice. It wasn't what I wanted to hear. But this morning you said almost the same thing. I calmed down after you left and thought it through. The letters, your walk to the docks—none of that was so terrible. I'm sorry, I was much too hard on you. You've always shown good judgment when it counted. You've always been trustworthy. You were right, I do owe you more respect."

"Thank you," Amanda said.

"I'll demonstrate my respect for your judgment. You may invite him to call on you."

"Thank you, Father. But it doesn't matter now. It's too late." Amanda's voice became flat. "I told you this morning. Jed Langford is gone."

In spite of everything, she couldn't imagine anyone else moving her the way Jed had. Not now, not ever. The days stretching ahead of her would be long, dreary, and loveless.

But early Thursday morning, Kat was banging on Amanda's front door. In her rush, Kat had left her brand-new bicycle leaning precariously against the gate.

"I was doing an errand and I saw him go by!" Kat said breathlessly. "Amanda, Jed Langford is back in town!"

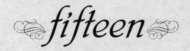

fifteen

"**P**apa sent me down to the docks with a package for Mr. Fiering." Kat was too excited to stop for a breath. "I saw Jed Langford walking toward Wharf Way! I couldn't wait to tell you!"

Amanda's hand went to her throat. "Are you sure it was him?"

"Of course I'm sure!"

Jed . . . "What was he doing?"

"Nothing. I mean, just walking with his hands in his pockets. Amanda, you look like you've seen a ghost!"

"What did he say?"

"Nothing. He didn't see me. He was too far off for me to say hello without running after him."

"Are you *sure* it was him?"

"For goodness' sake, I know what he looks like! Amanda, this is so *exciting*. He must have come back for you!"

"Oh, Kat! Do you think so? Where are my manners? Come on in."

"No, I can't. I have more errands, but I had to stop by and tell you! I bet you'll get a message from him any minute."

"Do you think I should look in the cave?"

"Well, *yes*," Kat said. "Amanda, what's the matter with you? You're acting *backward*."

"I'm just so surprised. I thought I'd never see him again. And now I don't know what to think. . . ."

"If not sooner, you'll see him in church on Sunday. He's sure to be there looking for you. Amanda, aren't you *happy*?"

"I don't know. He left without a word. That really hurt. And then I saw those whales and—Kat, I *hate* what he dreams about doing. I've been trying so hard to forget him."

"Well, he's back, so you don't have to forget him," Kat said. "You can't tell me you're not crazy about him."

"I guess I am, but I wish I wasn't. If he's going to be a whaler, I can't be with him. I can't."

Kat stiffened. "My father was a whaler. Do you hold it against him, too?"

"You know I love your father! It's different. I think

it is. I mean, it was a long time ago, so your father's not doing it *now*. So it doesn't have to be on my mind when I see him. But if Jed went to kill whales, I'd picture what he was doing all the time. I can't help it—it's horrible and I *couldn't* keep on caring for him." Amanda's eyes were wide and becoming moist. "What am I going to do?"

"Well, if it was me, I'd be with him anyway," Kat said. "Amanda, if it bothers you that much, tell him. He'll give it up for you and find another trade, that's all."

"Do you think he'd do that?"

"Look, he returned because he missed you so much. And realized he *loves* you. So he should sacrifice *anything* for the love of you!"

"That's a lot to ask."

"Changing trades isn't that difficult. This is so romantic! Amanda, can't you just *enjoy* it?"

"Do you really think he came back for me?"

"Of course," Kat said. "What else could it be, silly!"

What else could it be?

Amanda looked for a note in the cave that afternoon, and again on Friday and Saturday. There was nothing. But Jed had no way of knowing that she'd look there after all this time. Though he could have tried.

He didn't know Father had softened. He had no way of getting in touch. She'd have to wait until church on Sunday. One more day to go. . . .

If Kat was right, he had come back for her! He *was* back in Cape Light, wasn't he? Just like Kat said, he'd give up whaling for her and it would all be fine. Amanda Morgan and Jed Langford! Amanda Langford!

Amanda prepared for church with extra care on Sunday morning. She'd never been vain, but after all this time Jed's first view of her *mattered*. She brushed her hair, counting every one of the hundred strokes. Golden highlights shone among the light brown waves. She leaned closer to the mirror and examined her face. The long day she spent at the Durham Point beach on Tuesday had left a faint rosy glow on her cheeks. If people were forever telling her she was so pretty, today she could see it herself. Today she could *feel* it!

It was still August, of course, but heading toward fall and there *could* be a chill in the air. She'd take a chance and wear her burgundy wool dress, though it had long, tight sleeves. . . . Anyway, it was *lightweight* wool and it had that delicate crocheted edging around the neck and that elegant wide sash. It was the prettiest dress she owned, but more important, it was the one she'd worn to the barn dance so long ago. She wanted Jed to remember.

Thank goodness, the dress still fit well. A little tighter in the chest, because she'd developed a bit since last October, but it made her waist look tiny. She whirled around in front of the mirror and let the long, full skirt spin around her.

"Amanda? What's taking you so long?" Father called from downstairs.

Another quick peek in the mirror, a slight adjustment of the ringlets framing her face—she'd tied up those strands in rags overnight to get them right—and she was ready.

Jed wasn't in church yet when they arrived.

After she and Hannah were seated Amanda turned back often, waiting, expecting to see him come in late. But the service went on and on, and he still hadn't appeared. Finally, she forced herself to stop checking. No one would come in after worship was more than half over.

Jed Langford did not show up in church.

He had to know she was there.

He was back in town and made no effort at all to see her.

How could I have assumed so much? Amanda thought. Why did I get caught up in Kat's romantic imaginings?

Amanda was too warm. Heat rose in her face and her hair was sticking to the dampness in back of her neck. The tight wool sleeves itched. The stupid barn dance dress only added to her humiliating, crushing disappointment! She wanted to run outside, screaming, ripping everything off—but of course, she remained on the hard wooden bench until the last amen. Jed left without a word and that should have told me everything, she thought. How could I have misunderstood so much?

Amanda walked home with Father and Hannah. It was a brilliantly sunny day. A few of the trees had already turned scarlet and gold. The last of the daylilies waved bright orange along the road.

"She didn't come to church today," Hannah said.

Amanda was confused. Had Hannah picked up on her misery in the midst of all this natural beauty? "What do you mean by *she*?" Amanda asked.

"*Mrs. Cornell*," Hannah answered. "She didn't come to church today."

"Oh." Amanda had been too deep in her own unhappiness to notice. But Hannah had. Amanda glanced at her father's defeated expression. He most certainly had noticed.

All week long, even though they both put up a cheerful front, Amanda saw Father's sad resignation, which seemed to match her own. We're quietly licking our wounds, Amanda thought.

Only Hannah said what was on her mind. "Why didn't Mrs. Cornell come to church? Why don't we ever see her?"

"It's . . . um . . . it must be busy at the bookstore," Father answered. He looked so lost and wretched! Amanda couldn't bear it.

"But not on *Sunday*," Hannah corrected him.

Later, Hannah said, "Mrs. Cornell never comes to visit us. Doesn't she like me anymore?"

It broke Amanda's heart.

She couldn't do anything about her own unhappiness. But she couldn't let Father and Hannah continue to be miserable. Not if it was caused by her selfishness. Not if she could do something about it.

The bell tinkled as Amanda opened the door of the Pelican Book Shop.

She stood uncertainly in the aisle. Two ladies were

talking animatedly to Mrs. Cornell at the counter. Amanda saw Mrs. Cornell ring up a purchase, but the conversation seemed to go on and on.

Mrs. Cornell looked her way. "Hello, Amanda." She sounded surprised.

"Hello, Mrs. Cornell."

"May I help you with something?"

The two ladies were still there. It seemed they were settling in for the winter!

"No thanks. I'll . . . I'll just browse," Amanda said. She went blindly to the first table stacked with books and pretended to study the assortment. Oops, she seemed to be in the midst of veterinary medicine and cow diseases!

She moved over to another table. This one was piled with gardening books. Well, it was *possible* that she could be interested in gardening. She picked up *The Culture of Roses in New England Climates* and flipped through the pages.

She sneaked another look at Mrs. Cornell. Good, the ladies were leaving—but oh, no! Mr. Witherspoon stepped up in their place. She'd never thought of him as a reader, but there he was with two books. And he was opening one of them to read a passage to Mrs. Cornell.

She seemed constantly patient and good-natured.

Mr. Witherspoon, the expert square dancer at the barn dance . . . laughter bringing her and Jed together. She had to forget about that!

Amanda turned another page. Something about hills over the roots and straw cover for the winter . . . Mr. Witherspoon was handing over paper money and counting out coins. Mrs. Cornell placed the two books in a bag. Good, he was going. This was her chance, now or never, before someone else came in!

Amanda rushed up to the counter. "Hello, Mrs. Cornell!"

"Hello. I didn't know you liked to read."

"Oh, I do. A lot! My friend Lizabeth buys the new books and then we all read them. I mean, me and Kat and Rose."

"Yes, Lizabeth Merchant comes in often. So Amanda, you're interested in cultivating roses?"

"What?" Amanda was confused until she realized she was still holding that book. "No. Not really." She dropped it on the counter.

"What is it that I can do for you, Amanda?"

Amanda blurted it out. "Hannah misses you!"

"Oh. I'm sorry. Please, tell her to come here anytime. I always have some children's books and I'd love to see her."

"And Father is miserable!"

Mrs. Cornell looked at Amanda and said evenly, "I miss Roger, too."

"You didn't even come to church on Sunday."

"It seemed . . . awkward. I'll be back to church; it was just this first Sunday since—" She stopped and shrugged.

"You gave up on him awfully fast," Amanda said. "If you really loved him," she added with a hint of accusation.

"Amanda, I don't think I need to answer to you. Understand this: I've had a difficult time in my life and I finally reached some hard-won peace. I'm not about to struggle with your anger and hostility. I won't put any of us through that. A competition between us would tear your father apart, and there's no joy in that. There seemed no point in going on." Mrs. Cornell got busy straightening some papers on the counter. "He thinks the world of you, you know."

"Things had happened and . . . and I was mad. I'm hardly ever rude to anyone. I'm *always* polite . . . well, you don't know that. But I wasn't really mad at *you*,"

Amanda took a deep breath. "I mean the thing is, I had a mother. I don't think I can have another one."

"I had no intention of replacing your mother," Mrs. Cornell said. "That was the last thing on my mind. I hoped we would be friends."

"I've been on my own for a long time," Amanda said. "I mean, in charge of things by myself. That's what I'm used to."

"I've been on my own for a long time, too, Amanda," Mrs. Cornell said. "It would be an adjustment for me."

Amanda nodded. "It might not be easy."

"No."

The bell at the door tinkled and Mrs. Halloran came bustling in. The Pelican Book Shop had never seemed this busy!

Mrs. Cornell looked up, smiling. "I'll be with you in just a minute, Bertha." Mrs. Cornell pointed to a table in the corner. "Some new cookbooks came in. You might want to look them over."

They watched Mrs. Halloran wend her way to the back of the store.

"So where were we?" Mrs. Cornell asked.

"I don't know."

"Oh, yes. I was about to say, it seems we have a few

things in common. Three in fact."

"Three?" Amanda looked at her quizzically. "The whales."

Mrs. Cornell nodded.

"And being on our own?" Amanda asked.

"Right again," Mrs. Cornell said.

"And that's all." Amanda shrugged. "All right, what's the third thing?"

"We both love your father." Mrs. Cornell's face broke into a huge smile, a smile so engaging that Amanda could see why Father liked her so much. "That's why you're here, isn't it?"

"Yes. Yes, that's why."

"All right, then."

"Would you come back to him, Mrs. Cornell? Maybe come over after the store closes today?"

"I think you could call me Doris. As my friends do." Her big smile held. "Yes, after the store closes sounds like an excellent time."

⚞*sixteen*⚟

Amanda had just picked up the mail at the post office on Wednesday morning. As she turned onto East Street, she shuffled the envelopes in her hand. Bills for Father, a circular about subscribing to the *Saturday Evening Post,* a letter from Aunt Agatha way off in Ohio . . . She was passing the red-and-white pole outside the barbershop when she looked up.

Jed Langford! Jed Langford was coming out of the bakery!

Something fluttered inside Amanda's throat. She wasn't prepared! Stay, go. . . . Too late! He was walking straight toward her, heading in the opposite direction.

He looked startled. And embarrassed, as well he should! "Hello."

"Hello." She gave him a curt nod and kept going.

He continued past her.

Don't look back, she told herself, *don't*! But, as if a

177

magnet was pulling her, she couldn't resist turning back; one last glance, he'll never know . . .

To her surprise, Jed had stopped. He had turned, too, and was looking directly at her.

The normal noises on East Street disappeared. The clip-clop of the iceman's horse, little Willy Jackson whistling on his scooter, the rustle of the turning leaves on the maple trees, the little bell on the telegraph office door—it all faded away.

There was nothing left in the world but Jed's eyes. And her eyes, unable to shift away. Time seemed to stop.

"Amanda." Jed broke the spell. He took two steps toward her.

The curve of his lips. The angle of his cheekbones. He was still so handsome. She hadn't dreamed him.

"I heard you were back," Amanda said, as coldly as she could manage.

"I didn't get in touch because—" he began.

"It doesn't matter." Amanda interrupted. She shrugged. "I don't care. You didn't say anything about leaving, either."

"I guess I should tell you—"

"There's nothing to tell," Amanda said. "It makes no difference to me." She willed herself to turn and continue on her way. If she had a thimbleful of pride . . . But somehow, she was rooted to the spot. Pinned in place by his eyes.

"Seeing you again . . ." Jed drew in a quick breath. "I can't leave it like this. Let me talk to you."

Amanda steeled herself to refuse, but then he added "Please," so softly, and she couldn't help melting a little.

He looked around for a place to go. "The village green," he said. "For a minute. Please, Amanda."

She followed him across the lawn, past the statue of the lost fisherman, to a miraculously empty bench in front of the courthouse. The other two were taken, as usual, by elderly men, loudly arguing politics.

Amanda sat down, careful to leave a wide space between them. "Well?" she asked.

He scuffed his shoe along the ground. "Funny, we got so used to *writing* everything on our minds. That came easy to us, didn't it? It's harder to open your heart face to face."

"I have nothing to say."

"I do. When I left, it was all in a rush. I decided fast, that day after church."

"That day you yelled at me?" Amanda interrupted. The pain of it was still fresh.

He looked at her. "I wasn't thinking about how you felt. I was hardly *thinking*. I was just mad and humiliated! And tired of everything! All that disapproval from your father, reminding me over and over I wasn't good enough." His face reddened a little. "I didn't need a reminder. I knew I had nothing to offer. But if even my letters—only handwriting on a piece of paper—if even that—"

"It wasn't about you," Amanda said. "It was about me being too young."

"That's not true," Jed said. "It *was* about me."

Maybe Jed was partly right, Amanda thought. Father had called him "unsuitable."

"If you'd disobeyed him, given me half a chance . . ." Jed said. "I was praying for you to come through for me."

"I *couldn't!*"

"I know you couldn't." Jed gave her a crooked smile. "Always trying so hard to do right and worrying about the morals of everything—that's what makes you so special. I know that now. But that day I stormed home and got my grandpa to sign the permission slip—or else I would've forged it! I was going whaling and I'd come back with plenty of gold in my pockets, with more to offer you than your father or anybody, and then nobody could ever brush me away again!"

Amanda was dumbfounded. "Was *that* why? But why didn't you say anything?"

"Talk like that means nothing. I was going to come back to you with the real goods. I was too mad to think. I just took off."

Amanda stared at Jed. Of all the reasons she'd thought of, that was the one she'd never have guessed.

Jed opened the small white bakery bag he'd been carrying. "If I'd known I'd see you," he smiled, "I'd have got two." He pulled out a fat jelly doughnut. "Here, do you want it?"

"No, it's yours."

"All right, we'll share." He tore the doughnut in half. It turned out messy and uneven. Red jelly dripped on his hands. He held out the half that seemed to contain all the jelly to Amanda. "I wish it was diamonds."

Amanda took a bite. A fine dust of powdered sugar settled on her shirtwaist. Jelly oozed over her lips. "I never cared about gold or diamonds," she said.

He leaned over to her. With his finger, he wiped away the jelly around her mouth. Amanda almost jumped at his touch. He gently traced the curve of her lips.

He leaned forward a little more and somehow she

met him partway, not even realizing, and their lips met. His lips were soft and warm, and hot shivers rushed along Amanda's back. She clutched his rough, calloused hand. Her first kiss and it took her breath away. The loud voices of the men nearby, the dappled shade of the maples, the taste of strawberry jelly, and the grass-scented summer air became mixed up with the electric sensations running through her.

Surprised and confused, Amanda backed off. She re-established the distance between them on the bench. It took her a moment to find her voice, and even then, it came out husky and breathless. "You shouldn't have done that."

"No. I'm sorry. But you're so beautiful to me. . . ."

"There's something I have to tell you," Amanda said.

"Why does that sound like bad news to me?"

"That last day in church," Amanda went on, "I was going to say yes, I'd go on a whaler with you. And I'd wait forever until you could take me along. You didn't give me the chance. You stormed away before I could get two words out." She could still feel her burning embarrassment, with the whole congregation watching. "But I can't say that to you now. Everything is different. I wouldn't set foot on a whaler, not ever. This is serious for me, Jed.

Do you know about the whales that were beached at Durham Point?"

"I heard about them."

"I *saw* them. And I couldn't ever be part of harpooning them. Or being with someone who would do that."

"It bothers you that much?" he asked.

"Yes. It was a mother and a baby, and they broke my heart."

Jed gave her a long look. "You know how cute baby ducklings are, following their mama in a long line? Where do you think roast duckling with orange sauce comes from? Or lamb stew or—"

"Stop!" Amanda said. "I know that. But the whales, they were so strange and amazing and wonderful! And chasing them to the far corners of the world, invading their innocent ocean world—it's *wrong*! I couldn't in a million years be part of it. Anyway, if you become a farmer, I hope you'll be the kind that only raises crops."

"A farmer is the last thing on earth I want to be."

"All right, something else then. Anything else. It really matters to me. You can give me all the reasons and excuses in the world, but I won't back down." Amanda drew in her breath and watched for his reaction. "I can't help the way I feel." He didn't look angry; only sad.

"Jed—" She hesitated. "I have to ask you: Would you give up whaling for me?"

There was a long pause, with Jed deep in thought. Finally he spoke. "I have to give you an honest answer. No."

Amanda was shattered. Then there was no chance for them. He didn't care enough.

"Because it's the dream I've had for so long," Jed continued. "Because it's my family tradition—a proud and brave tradition, that made us *somebody*. Without it, we're nothing. Well, look at my father working in a cannery! So, no. I wouldn't give it up, not even for you."

Amanda sat still and hopeless, her hands folded together in her lap.

"But it kind of gave *me* up," Jed finally said.

"What do you mean?"

"I went up to New Bedford, looking to ship out. When I got there, I heard the price of whale oil had dropped once again. They were talking about oil fields discovered in Pennsylvania and electricity coming in all over. It's a lot cleaner than oil . . . And all those whalebone corsets getting made out of something softer. . . ." Jed didn't look at Amanda as he spoke. He kept his eyes on the ground.

"They said there was no reason whaling would ever come back like it used to be: the best days were over. There was only one whaler leaving out of New Bedford. It was an old tub. Didn't look like it'd withstand the first year of a two-year voyage. And with a ragtag, pick-up crew. I met a guy who had just quit from it. He said, 'You'll work like a horse, live like a pig, and have nothing to show at the end.' So my father was right all along. My grandpa was spinning an old man's dream of adventure."

"So you came back home," Amanda said.

Jed nodded. "With less than I started with. They filled my spot on the *Mary Lee*."

"Jed, I'm so sorry!" She couldn't stand the defeat in his face. "It had to be awful for you. I guess . . . I guess I'm glad you're not on a whaler, but I'm so sorry."

"You can't be glad and sorry at the same time, Amanda."

"Yes I can. I don't want you to feel bad."

"I'm all right. There are good parts to being home." He tried to force a grin. "My ma's apple brown Betty, for one, and I hear my goat missed me."

"You didn't try to get in touch with me. Not once since you've been back." It was hard for Amanda to say it out loud; it made her throat ache. She had been so hurt!

Jed faced her. "No. Because nothing's changed. My father could maybe get me work in the cannery or I might find work at the docks, swabbing decks again. Without whaling, I'm nothing. I've got nothing to offer you. Nothing to face down your father with. Nothing to even dream about. Zero."

"Don't say that, Jed, that's not so!" Amanda insisted. "You were brave enough to go all way to New Bedford! That same courage will lead you somewhere."

"I don't know. I'm scared I'll wind up like my father."

"I don't know your father, Jed, only what you wrote me about him. But you said he had no spirit and was afraid of change, and you're not anything like that. I know *you*, and nothing's going to keep you down, not for long."

"You think so?"

"I *believe* in you! Maybe you only need a little time between one dream and another."

He turned to her. "I'd sign on in a minute if whaling ever becomes profitable again. I can't promise you I won't."

"But that's very unlikely, isn't it?" Amanda said.

He nodded.

"I don't think it'll happen," Amanda said, "so maybe I can accept that. I'll try not to worry about something that's unlikely."

"Nothing's changed, Amanda," Jed said softly. "I don't think I'm willing to only catch glimpses of you in church. And look for notes tucked secretly into a cave. I swear, I didn't know I could care so much. You turned me upside down. But it's not good. Not for me and not for you. I can't ask you to sneak around, because that's not who you are, but—"

"But everything has changed. It has!" Amanda gave him a radiant smile. "My father and I . . . well, we've come to a new understanding. He promised he'd respect and trust my judgment. And . . . do you know Mrs. Cornell at the Pelican Book Shop?"

"I know who she is."

"She and Father are keeping company. She's softened him, Jed, and made him see he was much too protective. Things *are* different!"

"Are they?"

"Yes! And you know, I agree with you about those glimpses in church and the notes in the cave. That's not the way it should be. Jed, could we start all over? I mean, from the very beginning? As if—as if we've just met. And

I'm inviting you to visit at my house. And we'll get acquainted. And then we could see how it goes. I mean, if you want to, Jed."

"I guess we could see how it goes," Jed said.

"As a matter of fact, my father is home now, waiting for the mail. Come home with me! I'll introduce you and— We'll have to stay in the parlor. Oh, I didn't tidy it today! And my father will be within earshot, chaperoning us . . . like it should be. I never wanted to be Juliet!"

Jed followed Amanda home and she felt the apprehension in his every step. When they reached the front door he held his ground, though there was no telling what would happen next. He was brave to be going this far for her, and she was suddenly scared.

Amanda opened the door and stopped in the foyer. "Father?" she called.

She heard his footsteps come down the hall.

Please, God, she prayed, let Father truly come around. Please don't let Jed be humiliated again. She couldn't let Jed go through that! Maybe she'd made a terrible mistake. . . .

Father came into view. He stared at Jed, startled. Jed stared back, his face a careful blank.

"Father," Amanda said. She struggled to raise her

voice above a whisper. "This is Jed Langford. He's come to visit."

For a long moment, Amanda's pulse pounded crazily.

Father didn't quite smile, but his expression was not unpleasant. Finally he said, "Please come in, Jed."

Amanda's smile grew and grew.

~seventeen~

Father and Doris Cornell became engaged at the beginning of September. At first they planned a small gathering in the Morgans' parlor, but too many people wanted to come. They decided to move the party to the church hall and churchyard, but soon realized that the many well-wishers would overwhelm even that space.

Father is so loved, Amanda thought proudly, and he deserves to be. All the people he'd helped, counseled, and guided over the years wanted to share in his happiness. Doris's friendliness and the lively book chats that she ran at the Pelican Book Shop made her a popular personality in Cape Light, too.

Doris has made a wonderful difference, Amanda thought. The Morgan house rang with laughter now and Hannah was blooming. The only problem left was where could they throw an engagement party that would allow everyone in town to celebrate with them?

Kat's father came up with the answer. "How about a good old-fashioned New England clambake?" Mr. Williams suggested. "Cape Light hasn't had one in a long while. This Indian summer weather is perfect and we can use that strip of beach below the lighthouse. . . ."

It was a fine idea, Amanda thought, but what if they were rained out? Everything else had worked out perfectly so far, absolutely *everything*, so she had to have faith that the unpredictable September weather would be on their side, too.

It certainly was, Amanda thought as she looked around the sandy strip at Durham Point. Saturday night, September fifteenth, was unseasonably warm and clear. Everywhere, candles flickered in hurricane lamps. A three-quarter moon surrounded by dazzling stars sailed in a dark, velvet sky. Almost the harvest moon. Amanda glanced over at Jed and smiled.

Jed leaned on his shovel, wiped his forehead, and smiled back. He was with Chris Merchant, Mr. Williams, Mr. Alveira, Dr. Forbes, Mr. Baxter, and Mr. White. They were digging a deep pit in the sand. Farther down the beach, the little children, led by Todd and Jamie Williams, were picking up seaweed. Hannah came running with a huge pile of seaweed that threatened to spill out of her arms. Lizabeth, Kat, Mark, Joanna, and a bunch of other schoolmates collected rocks along the shore. The lamp in the lighthouse tower revolved steadily, illuminating the scene.

At a makeshift wooden table, Doris, Mrs. Forbes, Mrs. Merchant, and Mrs. Williams were among the many women setting up desserts. Amanda wanted to *see* them—she hoped Mrs. White's famous lemon meringue pie was among them—but all the pies, cakes, and cookies were carefully covered until later.

Father, Mr. Merchant, and Captain Caldeira led the men carrying wooden logs and kindling to the pit. Other men carried huge buckets of lobsters, clams, and mussels. Mr. Witherspoon and Mr. Thomas hauled crates of unshucked corn on the cob, silky tassels waving in the soft sea breeze.

Rose came up next to Amanda. "I've never been to a clambake before."

"It's an old tradition in Massachusetts," Amanda said. "The pilgrims learned how from the Wampanoags."

"Let's go closer," Rose said. "I want to see how it's done."

By now, the pit was wide and deep. Mr. Merchant

and Captain Caldeira placed the rocks at the bottom. Mr. Williams, Mr. Baxter, and Jed took the wood that had been collected and arranged it over the rocks. Then a fire was lit.

"They have to wait until the rocks are hot," Amanda explained.

When the rocks and wood were hot enough, they were covered with a layer of wet seaweed. Then alternating layers: lobsters, seaweed, clams, seaweed, mussels, seaweed, and then the corn with a final cover of wet seaweed.

"Now what?" Rose asked.

Kat and Lizabeth had joined them. "We wait while everything steams," Kat said.

"I'm starving!" Lizabeth said.

Delicious odors were already wafting over the beach.

Amanda's heart overflowed. All the good people of Cape Light were so full of love, participating in the pure happiness that radiated from Father and Doris. . . . There was Father now, with Jed. They looked comfortable together! Along with Chris, they were busy dragging crates of sarsaparilla soda onto the beach.

Amanda turned impulsively to her friends. "Let's go

up to our tower. Just for a minute, while we're waiting."

"All right," Kat said.

The four girls clambered up the narrow stone steps. In the tower they gazed out of the large curved windows.

"I wanted to see it from here," Amanda said, "and take everything in. I want to remember this night forever."

From high above, Durham Point spread grandly below her. The stars seemed close enough to touch. As the huge lamp revolved, it highlighted one scene after another. The ocean crashed into the jagged rocks along the shore, throwing white foam into the night. Well back from the spray, people were sitting on ledges on the rocks. Others laughed and talked in small groups on the sand. Little children ran and played. Steam rose from the pit and shimmered in the air. A bonfire near the shoreline was reflected, orange and red, over and over in the sparkling waves. "Thank you, God," Amanda whispered, "for all these bountiful gifts."

"It's so beautiful from here," Lizabeth said softly.

"Wherever I go, whatever I do, I'll remember it always," Rose said.

Rose is determined to go out west someday and fulfill her dream of a living on a ranch, Amanda thought. Kat will surely study art in a big city. Lizabeth will apply to medical school one day. That's extra hard for a girl, and she'll have to go wherever she's accepted. And I'll stay here in Cape Light. I don't want to live anywhere else in the world.

Rose sighed. "Summer's over and we go back to school on Monday. It feels like the end of something, doesn't it? Before the next chapter starts."

"I know. I was just thinking, the three of you are going to leave someday," Amanda said. "And I'll be left behind."

"A lot of girls would like to be 'left behind' with someone as handsome as Jed Langford," Lizabeth teased.

Amanda smiled. "We'll see. We're just at the very beginning."

"Seriously," Kat said, "we're *all* beginners. Absolute beginners, still finding our way. None of us knows what's going to happen next. But I know this will always be home base."

"Whatever happens, wherever you go," Amanda said, "let's promise we'll always meet here. Right here in our tower."

"Promise," the others echoed.

Lizabeth broke the spell. "The clambake must be

ready by now and I'm starving! I'm going to slather my corn with *pounds* of butter."

"All right, all right," the others laughed, "we'll head back down."

But before they left the tower, they stopped and clasped hands.

"The four of us, always," they whispered.

Read all the books in the
Girls of Lighthouse Lane series!

Pb 0-06-054343-4

Pb 0-06-054346-9

Pb 0-06-054349-3

Hc 0-06-054350-7

#1: Katherine's Story

Katherine is the daughter of the lighthouse keeper. She dreams of becoming a painter. But in 1905, a girl can't grow up to be a famous artist—can she?

#2: Rose's Story

Rose just moved to the town of Cape Light. She wants to fit in with her new friends, but Rose has a secret she can't share with anyone. . . . What will she do?

#3: Lizabeth's Story

Lizabeth is Kat's rich cousin who always gets what she wants. But Lizabeth soon finds out that money can't keep her from losing the most precious thing of all—and she is forced to take a look at the people and values that are most important to her.

#4: Amanda's Story

Amanda's mother passed away, and now Amanda keeps house for her minister father. When she meets a special young man, can she find the courage to be friends with him in spite of her father's disapproval?

■ HarperCollins*Children'sBooks*
www.harperchildrens.com

AVON BOOKS
An Imprint of HarperCollinsPublishers

 PARACHUTE PRESS

© 2006 Thomas Kinkade, The Thomas Kinkade Company
Morgan Hill, CA, and Parachute Publishing, L.L.C.